skin deep 2

skin deep 2 | MORE REAL-LIFE LESBIAN SEX STORIES

edited by

nicole foster

alyson books
los angeles

© 2004 BY ALYSON PUBLICATIONS. AUTHORS RETAIN THE RIGHTS TO THEIR INDIVIDUAL
PIECES OF WORK. ALL RIGHTS RESERVED.

MANUFACTURED IN THE UNITED STATES OF AMERICA.

THIS TRADE PAPERBACK ORIGINAL IS PUBLISHED BY ALYSON PUBLICATIONS,
P.O. BOX 4371, LOS ANGELES, CALIFORNIA 90078-4371.
DISTRIBUTION IN THE UNITED KINGDOM BY TURNAROUND PUBLISHER SERVICES LTD.,
UNIT 3, OLYMPIA TRADING ESTATE, COBURG ROAD, WOOD GREEN,
LONDON N22 6TZ ENGLAND.

FIRST EDITION: MAY 2004

04 05 06 07 08 **a** 10 9 8 7 6 5 4 3 2 1

ISBN 1-55583-777-8

LIBRARY OF CONGRESS CATALOGING-IN-PUBLICATION DATA
  SKIN DEEP 2 : MORE REAL-LIFE LESBIAN SEX STORIES / EDITED BY NICOLE FOSTER.—1ST ED.
    ISBN 1-55583-777-8
    1. LESBIANS—SEXUAL BEHAVIOR. I. TITLE: SKIN DEEP TWO. II. FOSTER, NICOLE.
  HQ75.5.S62 2004
   306.76'63—DC22   2003070338

CREDITS
COVER PHOTOGRAPHY BY STACEY HALPER.
COVER DESIGN BY MATT SAMS.

contents

introduction

This book is about as hot—and as real—as it gets. *Skin Deep 2* is the fifth volume of true-life lesbian erotica I've edited, and I've got to say, in all honesty, it's the best by far. What draws me to this collection more than any other is that the voices are so real, so different, in each story. And each story describes a sexual adventure that's very unique—and very, very hot! Take for instance, "My Sister's Flatmate," by Eva Hore, in which a woman watching her sister's friend get down 'n' dirty on video becomes the star of her own sexual show. Or Heather Towne's "Redirect," in which an aspiring law student eases a gorgeous, high-powered attorney out of her legal briefs. In "The Checker," Anna Craig shows us how to execute the perfect grocery-store pickup, and leaves us hungry for more than just a midnight snack.

Girls, this is a fabulous, fun, sexy book, so I won't waste any more time blabbing away here. (Does anyone ever read introductions to erotica anthologies anyway?) So let's cut to the chase and turn to page 1. I guarantee you won't be disappointed.

To lesbian sex! And lesbian love! Oh, and did I mention lesbian sex?

—Nicole Foster

after hours | kate o'neill

"This is crazy," I said.

"Shut up and kiss me," Casey said back, then my lips were captured by hers and I couldn't help melting, even though I was deathly afraid we were about to be found out and arrested, or at the very least fired.

Casey, my lover of five years, and I worked for the same company in Chicago but on different floors. When she picked me up at 6 that Friday night for dinner, we were already going down in the elevator when she told me, with this funny little grin on her face, that she forgot something in her office. Being the loving girlfriend I am, I went back up with her rather than wait in the car. The second we walked in her office, though, instead of flipping on the lights like I thought she would, she yanked me inside, shut and locked the door, and pushed me into her desk.

"Case—what the hell?" I managed to get out before she was on me, her hands finding my breasts, her lips nibbling at my neck.

"Oh, this is just a little adventure I've been planning. A fantasy I've had."

Casey likes to treat me every now and then, and she's wildly fond of surprises. So when I started to kiss her back, I just let go and went with the moment.

"Mmm—a little after-hours office romance," she purred into

my ear, which she then proceeded to tongue. I felt a rush of warmth from my head to my cunt, which was beginning to throb in that little way that told me this was going to be a good one.

"Up, here you go," she said, pulling back a bit so she could hoist me onto her desk. "Oops—let me clear that off."

With a sweep of her hand she brushed the entire contents of the desktop to the floor.

"Casey," I said in feeble protest, but she was on me again, and again I let myself surrender to the experience.

"Lie back," she ordered in a soft, dangerous tone. I could just make out her features in the streetlights that glowed in through the windows. *Avaricious* and *intent* might be two words to describe her expression, and that thrilling rush of pleasure surged through me again. Oh, yeah, this was going to be really good. Maybe I was starting to be less afraid of the possibility of anyone discovering us. In fact, that thought sent another zing through me, so I eagerly leaned back until I was prone on her desk.

"Now, let's see," she said thoughtfully. Slowly she rolled and tugged and pushed my tight little work skirt up my legs until it was bunched around my waist. My panties were already getting slicked up. Carefully she ran her fingertips under the top of my panty hose, then let them snap back, making me jump. With a smile I could just see in the half light, she pulled the hose down, under my ass, down my legs, stopping at about knee level.

"Hey," I whispered, "no fair. I can't move my legs enough." She laughed and bent forward to breathe a single hot breath against the crotch of my panties, then she slowly inhaled.

"Oh, Kate, you smell so good," she said in a serene voice that was barely laced with urgency. "Spicy, creamy, so delicious. I can't wait to dip my tongue in you and taste all of you, suck you up, swirl my tongue around and around, trying to get every last drop, feeling you drip down my chin." I thought my heart would catapult out of my chest as I listened to those words. "Lift your hips," she said firmly.

I did so, feeling a sweet ache centered somewhere just over the area she was describing, making me push my hips higher than was strictly necessary for her to slip off my panties. I heard her chuckle.

"Impatient, huh? Then let's get right to work." My lover bent her head down between my legs and did exactly what she said she was going to do. I felt her tongue dart in and out of my swollen lips, then linger for a long taste, then leave to trail wet kisses down my thighs and over my stomach. I gasped and arched my hips more and put my hands on Casey's head, pushing her onto me even harder. I heard her muffled chuckle before her lips started sucking at my labia, her tongue teasing my needy little clit. The sensations rippled over me like tiny wavelets in a pond, steadily building and rising.

"You know," Casey said, lifting her head for a moment, her voice a silky flow over my ears, "I could hold you like this for a very long time—just sucking, and teasing, and barely licking, keeping you right at the edge, not letting you fall over it, just—"

"No!" I said, and my voice sounded desperate. I could just see Casey's teeth as she flashed another wicked grin. "Please, let me come, please." I clenched my jaw to keep myself from begging. The wavelets were turning into a crashing tide.

"Well, perhaps," she whispered, and she bent her head down onto me again. Her tongue fluttered against my clit, little tiny flutters like a butterfly's wings, and I imagined the iridescent little things flapping against me, soft and pearly and smooth, slowly increasing in tempo, until I began to tremble and rotate my hips in that ancient rhythm against my lover's caress. She used her lips to plant little kisses on my sensitive skin in between the flutters, causing me to catch my breath in my throat and groan out unintelligible words into the stillness of her office. At that moment anyone could have walked in and I wouldn't have cared. In fact, I would've invited them to join in.

"Now, Kate," she paused long enough to murmur. "Now, my love. Come now." With a huge shudder and the feeling that the universe had just rained down all its bounty onto my galloping clit and the rest of my skin, I came so hard I thought I saw thousands of butterfly wings glowing against a velvety darkness. I bit my lip to keep from crying out and pushed Casey's head hard against me so she could feel the throbbing, could know the strength of what she had made me feel. My hips quivered and lifted again into the air, my fingers clenched the short strand of Casey's hair, and I banged my head against the wall behind the desk because I had slid back too far.

Very slowly the rush spiraled down, circling more and more gently until it stopped, leaving me in a sweaty glow and with a leaping pulse in my neck. Casey stayed until the last throb then lifted her head and maneuvered onto the desk with me, where she held me as best she could and rubbed my head, although I barely noticed that I had smacked it. We lay quietly, listening to the faint sounds of traffic from the city streets far below, which I had forgotten about entirely.

"So," Casey finally said, "like my little fantasy?"

"Uh-huh," I said into her shoulder.

"Now, I wouldn't want you to accuse me of sexual harassment," she said, running her fingers along my bare ass and hips, which drew an interested breath from me, "but what do you say about balancing out the deal? After all, no one knows we're up here, and we've got all night." I heard the amused note in her voice, and also the desire trembling beneath it.

"I'd say my dividends would increase greatly," I teased, and unhurriedly kissed her neck to demonstrate that our little escapade wouldn't be ending any time soon.

my sister's flatmate | eva hore

My sister Sonja was out of town for the weekend. She offered me the use of her shared flat to give me space from our parents; they didn't like my friends, wanted to know when I was going to settle down with a nice boy, and were concerned about my lack of interest in university.

I kicked off my shoes and lay on the couch, picking up the remote control. Nothing was on TV so I hit the video channel and accidentally pressed play. You can imagine my shock when I saw Sandra, Sonja's flatmate, and another woman making out on the tape. Rewinding the tape, I poured a drink, excited about what I was going to uncover.

"Oh, God, Melissa, you look fabulous," Sandra was saying when I pressed play. "Don't forget to work the camera—I want *all* of this on tape." I couldn't imagine Sandra having sex with another woman! She was always so sweet, and I don't know, nice.

"No problem," Melissa said, sitting down and crossing her long legs.

She was a gorgeous looking woman—very sexy.

"Come over here," Sandra said, patting her knee.

Melissa just stayed there.

"Do you enjoy being disobedient?"

"No."

"Then why haven't you come over here like I asked?"

"Sorry," she said.

She rose and stood in front of Sandra with her hands folded. "Bend over my knee."

Giggling, she did as told. Sandra pulled up her skirt and started to spank her on the butt. When she didn't respond, she spanked her harder.

"Ow!" she cried.

"That's what happens when you don't do as l say."

"You're hurting me," Melissa whined.

Sandra continued slapping her hand backwards and forwards, ignoring Melissa's pleas. "That's hurting," she said loudly.

"It's supposed to hurt," Sandra replied, lifting Melissa's skirt higher and pulling her panties down, exposing red cheeks.

I couldn't believe what I was watching. There was never any indication she'd be into something like this. I sat up and leaned toward the television, not wanting to miss a second. She rubbed her hands over Melissa's butt, caressing it with circular motions. Kneading the cheeks, she opened them, inspecting her, before sliding her finger toward her pussy.

Melissa moved her hands, trying to cover herself, but Sandra smacked them away. She squirmed trying to get up, but Sandra held her down.

I flushed. Was it because I knew I shouldn't be invading another person's privacy, or because I'd never felt so sexually excited?

"You're hurting me!"

"You shouldn't have put your hands there. Now I'll have to spank you with the ruler."

Melissa's butt grew even redder with each crack of the ruler. Sandra expertly slipped her panties down to her ankles. With her free hand she pushed Melissa's legs apart, giving herself a nice view of her pussy. I wondered how many times shed done this.

"Don't," Melissa said, trying to pull her legs back together.

"I said no talking," Sandra said, forcing her legs back open. She alternated the spanking, giving her one stroke with the ruler, then giving her butt a sharp slap. Occasionally she'd touch Melissa's pussy. I noticed Melissa's attitude shifting; she began pushing her butt up seductively, encouraging Sandra.

Oh, God, this was fabulous.

"Ow," Melissa suddenly squealed in pain. "Stop it. My butt's going numb."

"Shut up!" Sandra commanded, hitting her hard on the pussy. "Shut up, or I'll do it again."

Melissa stopped complaining and started moaning, making whimpering noises. The smack on her pussy made her open her legs wider. I couldn't tear my eyes away.

"I think you like this," Sandra said chuckling. "Do you think I need to punish you some more?"

"Yes," she whispered.

"What?" Sandra asked sternly.

"Yes. I need you to punish me more."

"Come on, stand up for me," she said, smoothing Melissa's skirt over her naked butt. "That's good. Turn around and take off your skirt."

I couldn't believe Sandra could be so assertive. She always seemed so gentle. Melissa had a sly smile now as she took off her skirt. Sandra turned her around, caressing her body.

When she was facing her again Sandra gently kissed her stomach while her hands traveled slowly downward into Melissa's pubic hair.

"Oh," Melissa gasped.

"You've got red hair there. And I thought you were a natural blond. Oh, and a little farther down there's some pussy lips. Hmm, it's a nice pussy, isn't it? Come and let me see the rest of you," Sandra said, moving her hands under Melissa's blouse.

Melissa undid each button, teasing Sandra as she went, pouting her lips and looking up at her through her lashes. Her blouse dropped to the floor; she stood there in only a white bra. She certainly wasn't shy now.

Sandra ran her fingers over the lace on the bra and forced her breasts up so they hung out over the top. "God, you're beautiful. Such lovely breasts." She gave the nipples a quick suck.

Melissa ran her hands down her stomach, then separated the lips, slipping her fingers inside. She leaned back against the desk and opened her legs, showing everything to Sandra, who knelt down, running her tongue over Melissa's pussy.

She stood then, fondling Melissa's breasts. "You like being good, don't you?" she said, unclipping her bra and letting it fall to the floor with the rest of her clothes.

"Yes," Melissa said.

I was mesmerized, and my own pussy started to throb.

"Lean over the desk so I can spank you some more."

Melissa didn't hesitate. Totally nude, she leaned on the desk with her butt twitching in the air, her feet slightly apart. Sandra produced a switch from her desk drawer. It looked like it was made of bamboo. She started to whip her.

"Oh, don't," Melissa said, flicking her hair around and looking at Sandra with her tongue running along her top lip. She didn't sound too convincing.

Smirking, Sandra spread Melissa's legs wider so she could see her pussy and started whipping a bit harder. Melissa, shocked by the force of the hit, put her hands behind to protect herself again.

"I told you not to do that, didn't I?"

"I'm sorry, but you're really hurting me."

"It's supposed to hurt, but I think you like it."

"No, I don't," Melissa said.

"I can see your pussy," Sandra said, rubbing her hand over it. "Hmm, yes. You're enjoying it."

"No, I'm not, honestly."

"Well that's not what your pussy's telling me. Look, it's

getting really wet now," she said, slipping in her finger. "Oh, yeah, really wet."

I watched as Sandra lowered her head to lick the welts. She ran her tongue over them, stopping just before her pussy. Melissa was up on her elbows now, pulling at her breasts, teasing the nipples to make them erect, pushing her butt into Sandra's face, lifting it higher, trying to get her to put her tongue inside.

Sandra stood then and looked down at her. "That's one hot butt," she said, laughing, pinching each cheek.

Sandra told Melissa to stand, then helped her up on the desk. She knelt so Melissa's pussy was level with her face. Sandra then smacked her thighs with her hand. She alternated between smacking her and giving Melissa's pussy a long lick, from her clit all the way up to her hole. Melissa was gyrating her pussy into Sandra's face, begging for more.

With her free hand Sandra undid her slacks and they fell to her ankles. She kicked them off her feet and I saw she wasn't wearing underwear. She covered Melissa's pussy with her mouth, nuzzling and sucking as she removed her shirt. Now they were both naked.

Sandra had her face smothered in Melissa's pussy. She bent over, grabbing her breasts. Melissa's head flung upwards, her breathing coming in gasps.

Sandra held Melissa firmly in the position as she pulled out a huge black dildo from a desk drawer. She then resumed smacking her thighs. It looked like Sandra had broken the skin, but Melissa was oblivious to it.

"Spread your legs and do what I tell you," she demanded.

"Oh, yes. Anything."

She parted her cheeks, rubbing the dildo over Melissa's pussy. She was wetting the dildo, teasing her pussy by just putting it in a fraction and then pulling back.

"Fuck me. Oh, please, fuck me now," Melissa begged. She turned around and I could see tears flowing freely.

I squirmed on the couch; my own pussy was throbbing, wanting some attention. I crossed my legs, but that only made it pulsate more.

Sandra grabbed her pussy hard. "Hmm, you like me punishing you, don't you?"

"Yes, yes," she said in between sobs.

Sandra grabbed her hips firmly, pulling her hard toward her, then plunged the dildo straight into her pussy. She thrust deeper and harder, causing Melissa to scream out for more.

"Quickly," she commanded. "Turn around and sit on the desk with your legs wide open."

Melissa did as told, and I knew why; from this angle I could see her pussy completely. Sandra certainly knew how to work the camera. I wondered how many times she'd done this.

Melissa was whimpering, begging for it. Sandra stood beside her, roughly pushing and prodding her pussy. She started to smack it with her hand. Melissa bucked her hips wildly, throwing her legs farther apart so that they were hanging off the side of the desk.

I was getting more and more excited. I moved my hand down inside my panties and felt my pussy. It was wet. Really wet. I slipped a finger in, then another as I opened my legs on the couch to find my clit. It was already hard. I rubbed it quickly.

I watched, fascinated with what was going on, even giving my own pussy a smack to see what it feet like. I felt myself starting to swell as the blood rushed into it. I moved my panties down and rubbed my clit harder, getting hotter and hotter. I finger-fucked myself, reaching a high I'd never felt before, as I watched the two of them on the screen.

Sandra turned her around, slammed her face down on the desk again, pulling her legs wide apart, and ramming the dildo into her hole. Melissa was delirious, matching her thrusts as she plunged it into her over and over. I frantically massaged my clit to an amazing orgasm.

Finally, she pulled the dildo out of Melissa and made her stand. Then Sandra lay on her back on the desk with her legs spread wide. "Eat me!" she demanded.

Melissa threw herself into Sandra's pussy. Then she spread Sandra's pussy and fucked her ferociously with the dildo.

"Oh, yeah, baby. Give it to me. Harder. Come on, harder."

My pussy was saturated now; the back of my skirt wet from my own juices. I rubbed furiously at my clit, harder and harder, until there was no energy left in me to do it again. I collapsed back onto the couch, breathing hard.

When I looked back at the screen Sandra had moved off, out of range, while Melissa lay there bruised, legs still wide open. I quickly pulled my panties up, covering my saturated pussy. I couldn't believe what I'd just done. I'd never enjoyed masturbation so much before.

"Having fun?" Sandra asked, interrupting my thoughts.

I jumped, embarrassed at having been caught. I realized from her casual stance that she'd been watching me. I didn't know what to say. My face was burning, and I flushed all over.

"You looked so sexy just now," she said, coming close to me. "I'll bet your pussy's on fire."

It was, but I wasn't going to tell her that. I didn't know what to say or do. I was still a virgin, but at least now I knew why I wasn't interested in finding a guy.

"Come here," she commanded as she grabbed the back of my head with one hand and pulled me closer into her body. I tried to pull back, but she held me even tighter, breathing into my ear as she kissed my neck. I gasped when I felt her hand lift my skirt. Forcefully she tore off my panties, the elastic leaving a stinging sensation.

"Don't," I said, shocked but aroused.

"Hmm, that's not what your pussy's saying. I was watching you enjoy yourself here on the couch. I think you might enjoy a spanking too."

"Please don't," I whispered, hardly able to speak over a stirring deep inside me.

She pushed me back onto the couch, and I tried half-heartedly to fight her off. I'd never made love before and didn't know how to go about it.

When her mouth covered my pussy I came immediately. I tightened my knees around her head, holding her close to me, not wanting her to stop. Her hands traveled up my body and she slipped them under my blouse and into my bra. Her fingers kneaded my breasts, pulling at the nipples.

"Oh, God, Sandra," I breathed.

"I've always wanted to make love to you," she mumbled.

I grabbed her head and pulled her mouth up toward my own, tasting myself as I kissed her passionately.

We tore off each other's clothes and went down on each other, sucking and licking, exploring and massaging. Then she rose above me, slowly making her way to that same drawer and brought out a dildo, which she strapped onto herself. She grabbed both my hands and held them over my head while her other hand pushed my legs apart as she groped for the dildo, rubbing my pussy with it before she pushed inside me.

I screamed out in pain as it tore into my hymen.

"You're a virgin?" she asked, shocked.

I nodded. She discarded the dildo and replaced it with her fingers. My body was on fire as they slipped in and out. Sandra looked down at me knowingly, a smile crossing her beautiful face.

God, it was heaven.

My eyes closed in ecstasy only to quickly fly open as I felt the sharp sting of pain as she slapped me hard on the thigh.

"Stop it! I don't like it," I said as she slapped me again.

"Yes, you do. Oh, yeah, you like it all right."

"I don't really…" I was enjoying it, but I didn't want her to know. Slapping me on the thigh was one thing, but whipping me was definitely out of the question.

Her hand slid down to my groin. Her thumb stroked downward, massaging as her fingers opened my lips wider, rubbing my clit, teasing it. She rolled me over on my stomach. Her hands caressing my cheeks, pulling them apart, gently running her fingers around my hole, tickling it. I felt light slaps in between caresses getting harder and harder.

My pussy twitched as the stinging sensation turned to pain. I got excited as I remembered how she'd smacked Melissa, remembered the look of sheer pleasure I'd seen on her face. Now I knew why.

I pushed my butt high up in the air, beckoning her to my pussy. Her fingers slipped inside as she continued to smack. I was gripped by a powerful orgasm. I collapsed, my body shuddering as my juices ran into her hand.

"Oh, God, Sandra. That was fantastic."

"I told you you'd enjoy it," she said chuckling. "Come on, admit it."

"Well, maybe just a little," I laughed.

"Sure," she said, stroking my hair.

"Maybe next time we can get Melissa to join us," she said, sucking my breast while her hand explored me. I felt myself quiver. "You'd like that wouldn't you?"

"You won't tell Sonja, will you?"

"Why? You think she won't approve?" she asked.

"I, um, uh…" I didn't really know what I wanted to say.

"What do you think she's doing right now? Sonja's gone to spend this weekend with her girlfriend. She's a lesbian."

"What?" I stammered.

"She's a lesbian too."

"You're serious?" I asked incredulously.

"Very. She never told you because she thought you

wouldn't understand. We've just been waiting for you to realize your own sexuality. Now everything will be out in the
open. There'll be no more hiding."

I smiled.

"Come," she said, leading me to her bedroom. "There's
so much more I want to teach you, and we only have the
weekend."

hank, just hank | toni chen

A few months ago I went to my second drag-king show, where I had my first boning by a bona fide drag king. His name was Hank, Just Hank, and he wore baggy black jeans, orange Vans, a loose T-shirt, and sunglasses. Hank was the surfer-cowboy of the group who played it cool in the background to songs by Southern Culture on the Skids and the Violent Femmes.

Each king had his own personality: the leather daddy, the bespectacled academic daddy, the butch bottom, the Latino, the inked rockabilly boi, the white trash boi with the missing tooth, and Hank. Hank's shtick was dildo performance art; during the first show he tied fishing wire to his "purple marauder" and went fishing in a yellow mop bucket, throwing his line back in after he caught two plastic fish and then (after a tug and a yank) pulled out Barbie. Hank clutched Barbie to his chest and walked, smiling, off the stage. It was hysterical, and I was smitten.

During the second show, the emcee announced that Hank was going to paint portraits with his strap-on and asked if anyone would like to volunteer. My hand flew up, waving madly while my friends pointed at me. Hank smiled and nodded to the emcee, who chose me.

I sat on the stage while Hank moved his rubber dick around in globs of finger paint, then slapped it on a canvas to create a likeness of me (emphasis on *likeness*). After he was done, I held it up while everyone applauded, but when I turned around to thank him, he had already sneaked up the back staircase to the green room.

The paint was still wet, so I laid the picture down in the backseat of my Volvo, then rushed back inside a few minutes before intermission. I downed a shot or two, grabbed a pair of Coronas, and pushed my way around the room until I finally saw Hank's straw hat from a distance. He was talking with a tattooed daddy in chaps and a wife-beater; for a moment my resolve faltered. Perhaps Hank wasn't quite what he appeared—perhaps he dug rough trade, not skinny geek girls like myself.

Then I figured, *Screw it.*

I decided to open with something noncommittal, casual, friendly, coy: "Hey, Hank, that was so hot." Well, it was friendly.

"Thanks." He dipped his head down and blushed. Nothing cuter.

"Here's payment for the picture," I said as I handed over the beer. "So, um, what's your last name?"

"Hank, Just Hank. Well, I guess then in that case Hank is probably my last name."

I wasn't sure if he was kidding. "Yeah?"

"Yeah," he laughed, drinking half his beer in one gulp. "It's ironic, but crowds make me nervous," he said, looking around at the glitter and epileptic lighting. "Want to go up to the green room? We're each allowed one guest…"

"Sure," I answered, a little too quickly.

The green room was littered with crunched-up Camel packs, strips of facial hair, scissors, socks, and kings waiting for their next act. "Hey, Hank," the rockabilly boi smiled over at us. Hank grabbed my arm and led me out on to the roof, away from the snickers of his friends.

"Smog sure makes for pretty sunsets," he said when we found a fairly clean area on the flat roof to sit down.

I looked over and watched him gazing out over the city, his light brown sideburns and goatee perfectly matching his real hair color. I'm not quite sure what the appeal of the drag king is, really; it's not the masculine, necessarily. Maybe it's the taboo, the girl-boi. Oh, who knows, who cares—it's all gender-bending fun.

"How do you keep your facial hair on?" I asked him.

"This theatrical glue. Comes off pretty easily with cotton balls and rubbing alcohol, except on your upper lip. It's rough there."

"But you have a full goatee."

"I suffer for my art," he said with a smile.

"So what's in your pants?" I asked, not even attempting small talk about movies or George Bush's latest blunder.

"Well..." He downed the rest of his beer. "Usually socks."

"Socks?" I asked. "Where's the marauder?"

"He's too...excitable to wear all night long."

"I see," I said, then began looking around for discreet places to make out. I completely dig kings and have always dreamed of making out with one, and I don't know why, but I felt like Hank's invitation to the green room was his way of telling me that we were going to be boning on the roof before the second act. Or maybe that was the Jägermeister talking— those two shots I had were kickin' in, and I was feelin' randy and hoping soon to be feelin' Hank.

"I need to put him away soon..." Hank said in a low voice, never taking his eyes off mine.

"So you're wearing it now?"

"Check and see."

For being so shy in public, Hank certainly did find his *cojones* in private.

I put my hand along the inside of his pant leg. "Wait, come here," he said. Hank grabbed my hand and pulled me over behind the air-conditioning unit on the far end of the roof. "I'm not in any numbers until the last song, so we have some time. If you want to spend some time with me."

I stood facing over the city, my back to Hank, looking over the air-conditioning box that came up waist high. Hank reached his hands under my skirt and pushed aside my underwear to make room for his fingers.

He kissed the back of my neck and brought one hand up to gently rub my nipples through my powder-blue T-shirt. His hands were strong and steady, increasing pressure until he was rolling my nipples between his thumb and index finger. Biting the back of my neck, making his way inside my panties with his other hand. I leaned back, pushing his fingers inside me while I gripped the edges of the dirty metal.

I wondered what he looked like as a girl;then an odd image flashed in my mind of him fucking himself as a girl. Of me fucking him as a boi.

I felt his rubber dick against the inside of my leg as he moved a second finger in, pressing out toward my stomach to find my G spot. "Do that with your dick," I whispered. "Please..."

"Bend over," he ordered sharply. So I did.

Hank rested one hand on his cock, then slid it inside me gently. I felt myself open up. He began fucking me in one continuous motion while his other hand continued working on my nipples up to where he was twisting and pinching them. I sucked in a quick gasp, but I liked the pain, so I didn't tell him to stop. I banged up against the air-conditioning unit, not caring about the noise or the bruises as he hit my spot over and over again until I felt a tingling deep inside. "Do you like this?" he asked.

I moaned and rammed back onto him, wanting every bit of force as he twisted my nipples until they burned. "Harder...fuck me harder..."

I bent over more and braced myself while he pounded me over and over until I felt my belly tighten. I touched my clit while he hit me from inside, sending waves of heat deep inside me.

All the sensations jumbled in my head: my hand on my wet heat, his dick pumping deeper and deeper inside, his wetness under that dick. I wondered if the cock was positioned well enough to hit his clit. I hoped so.

I spread myself open a tiny bit so I could access my hard clit better, then clenched around his cock and grabbed on to the metal box as I came in waves. Finally, Hank slowed down and stepped back, tucking his rubber dick back in his pants.

"I knew you were hot," I said, still shaking and blushing.

Hank nodded and offered to buy me a beer. "Do you come to all our shows?" he asked. "Because there are a few different views of the city available from this rooftop."

"I think I'd like to see them all," I said, grabbing his arm. "Maybe I could even show you a few new ones."

"Maybe," Hank smiled from under his hat.

three wrongs make a right |
heather meara

The biggest perk of being a writer is that I can convince myself that browsing in bookstores counts as research. My problem is that I feel the same way about bookstores that most women feel about grocery stores: What you want to eat and what you want other people to think you eat are entirely different things. For me, Dostoyevsky is my bitter cabbage and lesbian science fiction is my secret cake.

That's why I slink around, hesitatingly looking for the sequel to *Dykes of Uranus*. When I find it, I pluck it off the shelf, desperate to find out if Lavinia Labiala will escape from the clutches of the evil Lord Masculinia. I'm so immersed I don't sense someone creep up behind me.

"Heather, right?" I hear a soft voice in my ear. I jump and slam the book shut. When I turn around I'm face-to-face with a woman so breathtaking she could have stepped out of the pages of lesbian *Cosmopolitan*. I look around to make sure she's talking to me, thinking my day might be looking up when the anvil hits, smashing down with the weight of a 10-ton boulder: I know who this woman is, and I don't know if this is a friendly encounter. I almost didn't recognize her because the last time I saw her she was naked, and most decidedly not for my benefit. It's Rachel, the reason Andy left me. Or rather, the woman who caused me to leave after I

walked in on them having sex on the afghan my mother cro-
cheted for Andy and I when we had moved in together.

"Hey," I say, hiding the book behind me. "How's it
going?"

"OK," she says. "You?"

"Fine," I say, thinking that if I act cool, she might go away.
I wonder if she really recognizes me or thinks I'm someone else.
I look down to avoid her eyes. Not a good idea. What I notice
instead is that she's wearing a pair of skintight red leather
pants. I recall that the last time I saw her legs they were
wrapped around Andy's back. I remember they had a perfect
pedicure. They look as good clothed as they did naked.

"Do you know who I am?" I ask.

She blushes but stands her ground. "Of course I know
who you are," she says. "I may be a home-wrecking slut, but
I'm not a bimbo."

"Oh?" I say, because I can't think of anything else.

"I know it's probably a little late, but I'm sorry about
that," she says, shifting around like she would rather be
somewhere else.

"Yeah, well, you weren't the only one in that room," I
say. "Andy has a way of luring people into bed."

"You know Andy and I aren't together anymore, right?"

"No, but I can't say I really give a shit," I tell her, which
is a double lie: I did know and I do care. I know because Andy
called me up for drinks two weeks ago and I was stupid
enough to go. Then after a night of drunken sex, she disappeared off the radar again.

"Well, we're not," Rachel says, stepping closer to me.

"Did she cheat on you too?" I ask.

"Matter of fact, she did," Rachel says, "but I can't say I
really give a shit." She laughs, tossing her head back, exposing the nape of her neck. Suddenly I have an urge to lean forward and kiss it.

"You shouldn't," I say, reaching out to grab her arm.

"She's an ass, and you're way more attractive, and on first glance probably twice as smart."

"Thanks." She shuffles her feet likes she's going to leave. But she doesn't. "I was always afraid you hated me," she says. "I mean with good reason, but—"

"I did," I say.

"Yeah. I guess I always hated you too."

"Thank you. That's a real boost to the ego."

Rachel blushes again. What is it about a woman blushing that turns me on? I think it's just too easy to picture them during sex: hot, sweaty, and glowing.

"I just hated the *idea* of you," she says. "I always felt like Andy was wishing you were still in the picture, that she only ended up with me because she got caught."

"Yeah, well, that's Andy for you. Always wanting what she can't have. She hasn't changed a bit."

"Have you seen her?"

"Yeah," I reluctantly admit, feeling strangely ashamed which is odd because you'd think I'd be gloating. "We're not back together. I mean, I saw her once and, well, you know Andy." I don't know why I'm telling her this.

"Bottle of wine, then 'I'm going to bed, you can come if you want,'" Rachel says.

"Something like that," I say, more than a little disturbed by her accuracy. "Except it was two bottles."

"Oh," she laughs. "You must have a higher tolerance than I do."

"For alcohol or bullshit?"

"For both," she says smiling. I find myself noticing the little specks of gold in her hazel eyes. We hold eye contact for an eternity before she ducks her head and looks away. "So, this is weird, huh?"

"Yeah," I mumble.

She shifts her weight from foot to foot. "What are you reading?" she asks pointing at the book in my hand.

"Oh, nothing." I try to hide it behind my back again, but she takes my arm and holds it where it is.

"Hmm. *Dykes of Uranus II*. Interesting choice."

"Actually, it's not mine."

"Oh?" she asks, sticking out her lower lip. "Whose is it?"

"Can I trust you with a secret?" I ask. She nods. "I'm undercover police. I was assigned by the feminist literati to wander around bookstores plucking bad novels out of people's hands."

"Is that right?" Rachel asks.

"Oh, yes," I say. "It's a very serious and depressing assignment. You should have seen the poor woman I took this from. Big bottle glasses, lavender muumuu, and dangling feather earrings."

"Hmm..." Rachel's fingers travel up my arm. The spot they touch starts to tingle. "Do you always have to respond when you catch someone with bad books?"

"Yes, ma'am," I say, nodding gravely. "I'm always on the job."

"Well, then," she says. "I guess you'll have to arrest me." I look at her and raise my eyebrows. She points to her basket on the floor. On the top of the pile in plain view is *Dykes of Uranus II*. I look at it, then back at her. She holds out her hands in front of me. "I guess it's your move."

"I guess it is," I say, and before I know what I'm doing I grab her wrists and lean to kiss her. Her lips are soft and warm; they taste like hot chocolate and ChapStick. I pull back a little to look at her. She's smiling. I want to kiss her again but instead, I pull away. "I'm sorry," I mutter. "That was wrong."

"The only thing wrong is that it didn't last longer," she says. Then she blushes again, a wash of red traveling all the way down to her collarbone. I wonder what it would feel like to kiss her there, at the hollow of her throat.

"Are you sure you don't need to arrest me?" she asks, tilting her head to the side. "I promise not to resist."

"I'll let you go this time. But if anyone asks, I'll deny it happened."

"Thanks. I'll try not to read anything else into that."

"Don't," I tell her. As she turns and walks away, I notice how strong and confident her walk is, that lovely combination of swagger and swinging hips. I'm tempted to run after her and beg her to kiss me again but I tell myself not to be stupid.

Instead I drop into a chair and open *Dykes of Uranus II*, but I can't focus on the words; I can't get Rachel out of my mind, her standing there tall and strong in her bulky winter coat, just thick enough to make you wonder what was underneath.

I lean back into my chair and close my eyes. I imagine Rachel sliding into my lap, reading softly, her lips blowing a soft air onto my neck as she speaks. I must've dozed off because suddenly I'm Labiala, leader of the *Dykes of Uranus*, gazing out at the horizon, watching the Masculinians approach at an alarming rate, skimming across the ground in hovercrafts made of lightening. Areola, my coleader, is by my side, except she looks exactly like Rachel. It starts to pour, and the rain cascades down on us as if trying to wash us away. I feel my leather bra and shorts tighten against my skin. Rachel/Areola is so close I can feel the heat flash between our bodies. "They're coming," I say, gesturing toward the horizon.

"I know," Rachel/Areola agrees, gripping my shoulders with her long, elegant hands.

"We're not ready," I shout above the thunder. "They'll destroy us. What should we do?"

"Nothing."

"Then what?" I ask. "Do we go out fighting?"

Areola shakes her head, sliding in closer. The rain streams down her breasts, pooling in her cleavage.

I look at her, wondering how anyone could be so beautiful. She starts to cry, her chest heaving up against the rain. This time

I can't stop myself from reaching down to lick at the water, letting my tongue find her nipples, which grow hard underneath my touch. Then she lifts my head and slides to kiss me.

She whispers into my ear, "I want to go out making love. I want to meet the goddess screaming your name."

We desperately rip the clothes from our bodies and fall, writhing on the muddy ground. My hands reach around her ass to dive deep between her legs as the thunder claps again and again and she shouts my name. Then through a dim haze I realize she's calling Alison, not Labiana, and the thunder is not thunder but someone rapping on the bookshelf above my head. When I open my eyes, Rachel is standing over me. I stumble back to consciousness, embarrassed to feel a slight wetness between my legs.

"You're still here," she says, sitting on the stool next to my chair.

"Yes, and apparently so are you."

"I came back to find you."

"You did?"

"Yeah," she says, sliding her tongue out to moisten her lips.

I walk over to her and she pulls me between her legs, pressing her knees tight against my hips so I can't escape. Not like I want to. What I want is to kiss her again, longer and harder, but I don't have the guts. "Your move," I say.

She grabs the back of my head and pulls me to her lips. Now they taste like peppermint and coffee. It makes me wonder if she tastes this good everywhere. At first, all I feel is softness, then her tongue grows forceful, darting in and out, licking my lips, the tip of my tongue, then reaching deeper. It's just the right combination of soft and fast, of light and hard; it makes me wonder what her tongue would feel like on my clit. There's a flood of heat between my legs.

"Let's get out of here," she whispers, without letting her lips leave my mine. I nod, running my fingers down the back of her neck and biting her lower lip.

Out on the street we desperately try to flag a taxi, but it seems like every cab is full. Finally one stops and we scramble in.

I slide into the backseat and Rachel climbs onto my lap. "Where are we going?" I ask as she turns around to kiss me.

"I have houseguests," she says, running her fingers across my chest, stopping to pinch my nipples.

"Shit," I say, remembering that my mother is still at my house. "So do I."

"We could do it here?" she laughs, nibbling my neck as the cab driver pretends not to watch in the rearview mirror.

"I'm sure it happens all the time."

"Hmm, I have an idea," Rachel says, kissing me again.

"I have a few ideas too," I add, sliding my hand between her legs. Even through the leather I can tell she's on fire.

"Hmm, good," she moans, sliding off my lap to kneel on the floor of the cab. "But I mean I know where we can go."

"Where?" I ask as she slides my legs apart. Her mouth hover inches from my pelvis.

"Let's go to Andy's," she says, biting the inside of my thigh. "I still have a key."

"Are you crazy?" I ask. "What if she comes home?"

"She won't. She works until midnight. That gives us at least six hours, which might be almost enough time."

"We can't," I say, but when she gives the cab driver the address, I don't try to stop her.

When we get to Andy's the doorman gives us an odd look. I don't know if it's because he recognizes us or if it's obvious that sex is streaming from our bodies.

The elevator has mirrors on three sides, and as we start up Rachel wraps her arms around me from behind. "I think we look good together, don't you?"

"Yes," I answer, "but not as good as we'll look naked."

"Maybe I'll take your clothes off here. She sneaks her fingers under my shirt.

"Are there still cameras in the elevator?" I ask.

"I think so."

"So the doorman can see us?" She nods. "Then I probably shouldn't do this," I say, turning her around, pressing her against the back of elevator, and lifting up her shirt to kiss her stomach.

"Probably not," she moans tilting her head back, exposing the stretch of neck from ear to collarbone. I move up to suck at the milky expanse of skin.

"Well, if you shouldn't do that, I definitely shouldn't do this," she says, turning me around and lifting me up to the railing running around the elevator's perimeter. She's a good five inches taller, so it puts her pelvis level to mine. She starts to press into me like she's ready to fuck. "Do you like that?" she whispers, and it is all I can do to nod yes. "Good," she says. "I can't wait to tear into you."

"Hmm," I moan because I can't get the words out. She reaches her hand between us and presses her thumb into my clit with a small but incessant pressure. Then she eases her pelvis away but holds me in place with her hands. "But I have some other plans for you first."

"Oh?" I say, squeezing my legs around her hand. "Tell me."

"Well, first, I'm going to lay you on the bed and I'm going to kiss every inch of your body, making a slow trail of kisses from your lips down to your pussy, and after that I'm going to lick you until you're hard enough to burst."

"I think I'm almost there," I murmur quietly.

"I hope not," she says when the elevator stops at our floor, "because then I'm going to fuck you until you come so hard you cry. And that's only the beginning."

"Don't worry. I'm insatiable. I'll break you before you break me."

"Oh, we'll see about that."

I grab her hair and pull her closer. When the elevator door opens, she laughs and pulls away, catching me just before I fall.

Rachel fumbles with the key outside of Andy's apartment and I almost turn around. "This is wrong," I tell her.

"Yeah," Rachel says without turning around. "But three wrongs make a right." She opens the door and pulls me inside. We stumble to the bedroom without turning on the lights.

Rachel pushes me back on the bed and I reach up to pull her onto me and the weight of her body feels amazing. "Hold on," she commands. "I want to see you. And I want you to see me."

She turns on the dimmer. Her skin looks golden in the shadowy light, as if it had been dipped in sun. I watch as she peels off her clothes, as effortlessly as breathing, stripping down to a red lace bra and panties.

"I see you," I say, looking her up and down, loving the soft rise of her belly, the gentle slope of her tight, full ass. Her hipbones jut out in sharp little points, like handles. I want to grab them and pull her to me.

Rachel comes back to the bed dancing slightly as she crawls on top of me. I look over at the bedside table where there's a picture of Andy and Rachel at someone's wedding. Andy's wearing a tux and Rachel is in a tight red dress. "Nice picture," I say pointing. "Looks likes she's not over you."

Rachel reaches out to grab the photo. "See the bridesmaid standing near the bar? Two days later Andy was all over her."

I hold her back with my hands. "So is this about revenge?" I ask.

"Maybe a little," she says, leaning in to kiss me. "And you?"

"Oh, for me it's all revenge." I wrap my legs around her hips. "And I guess it doesn't hurt that I'm really into you and you have me so incredibly hot."

"And that I'm going to fuck you until you come so hard you couldn't move if the bed caught on fire."

"Hmm," I say. "Then there's that."

"So, to Andy, is it?"

"To Andy," I toast.

I take the photo from her and toss it to the floor. When it hits, I hear the glass break. "Sorry," I say, as I run my hands down Rachel's thighs feeling her muscles tighten as she grinds her hips into me. "But I think she needs to let go."

"I think we all do." Rachel slides off me.

"Where are you going?" I ask, reaching out to draw her back.

She leans down to kiss me. "Don't worry—I'll be right back. Just close your eyes."

I close them. I hear sounds from the closet and then her footsteps coming back to bed.

"OK, open." She's wearing Andy's tuxedo jacket, bow tie and cummerbund and holds a long velvet scarf in each hand. "Luckily I know where things are."

I reach out to pull her onto the bed but she swats my hands away. "Not yet," she says, pushing me back onto the mattress. "Do you trust me?" she asks, and I nod because for some reason I do. She makes me close my eyes then wraps one scarf around my eyes and uses the other to tie my hands above my head as she hovers over me. She smells like a combination of lavender and Aveda.

"You smell like Andy," I say.

She puts a finger to my lips. "I am Andy," she whispers. "And while your eyes are closed I'm going to touch you like her and fuck you like her until you want me to stop. And when you're over that, do you know what I'm going to do?"

"What?" I ask.

"Then I'll take your blindfold off and we'll fuck again like us, and it will be even better because she'll be gone once and for all."

When she starts to touch me, it does feel like Andy, the way she traces her lips across my inner thigh, darting in and out to tease, then sliding her fingers between my legs, pressing the heel of her hand against my clit. It's strange we learn to fuck like the people we fuck. She slides down across my body and starts to lick me, her tongue a soft full pressure against my clit. My lips become engorged, and I thrust my pelvis up into her mouth. Her tongue flicks against me again and again, wet and warm; I bite my upper lip. I feel like I'm ready to explode, but I can't come. I don't want to come.

"Take it off," I beg. I want her to free my hands and my eyes so I can touch her and see her. I want rip off Andy's clothes and feel the entire length of her beautiful naked body.

"Why?"

"Because I want to fuck you and not her," I answer, and it's true.

"Good," she says, "because I want to fuck you too."

She unwraps the scarf from my eyes and unbinds my hands, then she shrugs out of the tux and throws it on the floor.

"Better," I sigh, sliding my hands underneath her bra to unhook it, watching her breasts fall free. When I slip off her underwear I can't stop myself from reaching up to slide my fingers deep inside her. She is drenched. "God, you feel good," I moan, flipping her over onto her back. Now it's my turn to explore her body. I kiss my way down the path of her stomach stopping at the mound of her pubic bone. I nuzzle it with my chin and lips before I allow my tongue to slip inside her. I've never tasted anything so wonderful. As I nibble and lick, I grow even harder. When I can't take it anymore, I slide myself up until my pussy is pressing against hers, thrusting.

"Like that, but harder," she moans, and I lean onto my hands to get more leverage.

Then she flips me over and moves into me, reaching her arm down to massage my clit until I feel like I'm about to erupt. It feels so good I start to cry.

"Are you coming?" she asks.

"Yeah," I gasp, "I'm coming."

"Good," she says, pushing into me harder. "So am I." Then we let go at the same time, and I come harder than I've ever come before. I feel the release of my orgasm streaming from me, making our bodies slick. Rachel collapses onto my chest, and I draw her to me tightly. Her body quivers in my arms. And she's right: I couldn't move if the bed were on fire.

"Thank you," I whisper into her ear. "Thank you."

"Thank *you*," she says, turning to kiss me. We lie there holding each other until just shy of midnight and then slip out, leaving the sheets tangled with our scent.

fucking for real | nairne holtz

When I was in my mid 20s in the early '90s, I hung out with a crowd of bad-ass women who were five to 10 years older than me. The kind of gals who had been eighty-sixed for throwing bar stools, or kicked out permanently for selling dope on Hell's Angels territory. I was the question mark in the group, the ingenue. I spent as much money on books as I did on beer. I made my living flipping burgers, but I also went to university. I had grown up in the same sort of neighborhood as these women, but I wanted to wind up somewhere else.

I met these women the way many other women in the Montreal club scene met: a one-night stand with Donna. Donna was more attractive than beautiful; there was something about her. She worked with her hands, making stained glass; she had a deft, sensitive touch. But she was also a paranoid, angry drunk whose relationships quickly dissolved. Unlike the other femmes, bisexuals, and "straight" women who slept with her, I became her friend. What I liked about Donna and her friends was that there were no rules. If I showed up in a dress, no one said I looked like a straight girl; instead, Donna would tell me I looked pretty.

I got involved with a friend of Donna's named Toni who was visiting from the West Coast. What happened between Toni and I wasn't exactly the thing dreams were made of, but she marked me as surely as if she'd had a tattoo gun. We met at a barbeque at Donna's. I had no expectations for romance, so I dressed casually in cords and a '60s paisley shirt.

Donna's apartment was long and spare, painted in cool colors and decorated with campy little dolls and promo posters for dyke nights. Donna introduced me to Toni as soon as I walked in.

Toni had a head-turning buff body. Her stomach and biceps were flat and hard as tin; she showcased them well in a tight black T-shirt. I thought she was an amateur weight lifter, but it turned out her ripped muscles were a result of working as a landscaper. She had a heavy, deliberative walk, long blond hair, and pretty features.

Halfway through the party, a woman was getting drunk and weird. She started describing being sexual abused when she was a kid. Every woman in the room flinched. We were all matches, struck and flamed by violence, nonconsensual sex or family lives saturated with selfishness and hatred, self-hatred. No one said anything, but I listened then chatted to this woman who was a living, running sore. After a while I managed to get her to turn a corner into normalcy. I didn't realize it, but Toni was watching me the whole time.

Donna called me the next day to tell me Toni had a crush on me. "She thinks you've got this good soothing energy." Was I interested? Would I come out with them that evening if I wasn't working?

Sure. She had a hot body, why not? I didn't care that Toni lived on the other side of the country, was more than a decade older than me, and shared none of my interests outside of going to clubs. I let Toni take me home the next night in a sea of booze and coke. I can't remember what we talked about, but I do remember dancing and the two of us pitching forward onto the floor at one point. I recall her saying in the cab that I wasn't her type; she usually went for women who wore high heels and a lot of makeup. I felt slightly hurt; it was like a high school reminder that I was more egghead than hot glamour girl.

I brought Toni to my place, since she was sleeping on Donna's couch. I rarely had sex with women at my flat because it was out of the way, up north in the garment district. I lived by myself on the third floor of an ancient triplex. It was cheap with beautiful moldings and columns in my bedroom. I had painted it all different colors—midnight blue, lavender, and ivory, then draped it with silk and East Indian cotton bedspreads. It was my little sanctuary. As soon as Toni and I got in the door, we headed straight to my futon. I crawled on top and began to kiss her neck. She made noises in her throat. I unbuttoned her shirt and licked her nipples until they were pale pink peaks, meringue on a pie. I took off her jeans. Her body beneath me was both smooth velour and rock-candy hard. I kept my own clothes on like protective fur but also because it turned me on.

Toni pulled her mouth from mine. "You're a top. That's so fantastic because women usually think I am, but I'm not."

I had never thought of myself in terms of "top" or "bottom." I tended to take care of other women's needs because I was too self-conscious to let women take care of mine. But what she said tangled with various memories: high school fantasies of being a man fucking a woman; daring a feminine lesbian friend who wasn't attracted to other feminine women to let me kiss her and having her say, "Hmm, so aggressive, not what I expected" in a pleased tone. It made me think of the dildo I'd bought but hadn't had the chance to use.

After we kissed and touched some more, I got up from my futon and opened my top dresser drawer. After rummaging around for a bit, I found what I was looking for: the pink silicon dildo and a soft black leather harness covered in flat silver studs. I slipped the harness on over my cut-off jean shorts and pulled the dildo through the silver buckle. Like guys who are virgins, I acted like I had done this a million times.

Toni's eyes gleamed. "I didn't expect this from you. You seem so serious and shy. This is great."

I felt faintly ridiculous walking about with this rubber wand, but the minute I plunged it into her and she moaned, my feelings of discomfort disappeared. She wanted me to rock into her so hard, I couldn't believe it. It was cool, though. It was something I had been waiting to do for a long time without realizing it. Screwing her made me sweaty and horny. I growled at her to come and she did. I'd never been to bed with a woman who could come just from being fucked. Vaginal orgasms weren't a myth. Interesting. That was my last coherent thought before I passed out.

The next morning, Toni woke me up at 7. She had tuned the radio on my boom box to a high-energy dance station and was rolling a joint.

"I used to be addicted to coke, but now I just smoke up every morning. It makes me less hyper," she said.

That was hard to imagine, since she was naked and shaking her hips like a gay boy to RuPaul. Toni was this interesting combination of sex kitten, blue-collar straight boy, and dancing queen. I offered to make coffee, but she wanted me to have sex with her.

Sex in the morning? Sober? I had only ever done that with one other woman, and that had been five years ago.

But I let her have her way. I remember being naked, lying between her legs and spiking the tip of my tongue along her cunt.

"Don't stop," she cried.

I eagerly continued. Her body rippled in response, and I startled to really feel something. Fear, inhibition, murky drunkenness, and guilt over my inability to repay love in kind, were pared away. Other encounters held flickers of this passion—I had even orgasmed with my first woman lover five years earlier—but fucking Toni had a raw naturalness I had never experienced. When Sylvester sang "You Make Me Feel

Mighty Real" I finally knew what he meant. Toni was tequila on the tongue, hot. I dipped my fingers into her. Her aromatic, musty girl smell was intoxicating. I licked her a little more, and she came in a shiver.

She wanted to touch me; I let her. She licked the pink plums of my breasts. She traced my cunt with her fingers.

"Am I wet?" I asked. I spoke shyly, but I meant it to be saucy. When she licked me I was a ring of crackling heat. I didn't figure out then that if I ordered someone to go down on me, it freed me. It allowed me to be a nasty, greedy bitch who could come over and over again. But Toni and I, we had the right kind of dynamic. Femme top and butch bottom, although I didn't have the language for it at the time.

Outside the bedroom, our connection rapidly disintegrated. After I made her breakfast, I walked her to the Metro. She kept leaning into me and trying to hold my hand, acting like we were in love or something. We had sexual chemistry, but since she lived across the country I saw no reason to try to wring more out of us. I noticed some old women staring at us, and I'm sorry to say I dropped Toni's hand as if it had seared me. She didn't say anything. I called her later that day during a break at work to see if she wanted to go out, but she said, "This old lady needs to get some rest." We agreed to meet the following evening.

Things got off to a bad start when I showed up with my friend Angela. Toni immediately asked her where she was from.

"Ottawa." Angela's face became a hard egg.

"Where are your parents from?" Toni persisted.

Angela rolled her eyes. "China."

"I've traveled to Asia," Toni began.

Angela cut her off by walking away to the bar.

I was stricken. Toni had been rude, bordering on racist. At the same time, I recognized that my university education had given me the tools to unlearn attitudes I had grown up with, and Toni and Donna hadn't had the same opportunities.

Toni and I danced after that, but we weren't a good fit. I stomped my boots and moved around a lot while Toni swayed her hips. A slow song came on and we moved into each other's arms. I relaxed a bit, but then Toni twisted her tongue into my mouth. It felt too sudden and intimate. I needed to work up to feeling close to her again. I guess she sensed it, because the next thing I knew she left me to get a beer from the bar and didn't bother to ask if I wanted one. I saw her bum a cigarette from a woman and give her a long look. She asked another woman for a match and began talking to her.

I went to the bathroom, then headed to the bar where I felt someone grab my arm. It was Angela. "I think Toni found herself a honey." She jerked her head dismissively in Toni's direction.

Sure enough, Toni was nibbling the neck of the woman who had given her a light. The woman was a baby, 22 at the most, with big hair and lots of makeup. I twitched with jealousy, little snakes in my stomach. But a deeper part of me felt relieved. Toni overwhelmed me.

Toni glanced up and met my eyes without a trace of embarrassment. It seemed as if she was challenging me to respond to the situation in some dramatic and intense way.

"What does she want from me?" This was so not my style.

"She wants you to stomp over there, grab her..." Angela gripped the collar of my shirt dramatically in her fist, pulling me toward her, "and tell her, 'Bitch, you're coming home with me.'" She released my shirt. "But she's an asshole, so you should just forget about her."

I ignored Angela's advice and walked over to Toni. The young woman she was with dug a compact mirror and lipstick from her purse. She gazed into the mirror and fixed her lipstick by wiggling her lips. I childishly assessed her physical appeal against my own and smugly concluded that I had a nicer body. I placed my hand on Toni's waist. "I need to talk to you."

Toni immediately followed me a few feet away from the woman.

I cut to the chase. "Do you want to go home with me or her?"

"I don't know," Toni paused, determined to milk the scene for the maximum attention and drama. "Both?"

"Forget it," I snapped. "I don't find her attractive."

"Her, then." Toni tapped my breastbone. "You don't pay enough attention to me. I need that."

In that moment, everything between us crumbled like pick-up sticks. I couldn't give her what she wanted. Later that week, after she left, Donna told me Toni had been the baby of her family, spoiled by all but especially by her mother, who had died when Toni was a teenager. Donna said that when she first became friends with Toni, she would miss her mom so much that she'd periodically hyperventilate.

Angela and I left the bar together, and she seemed more outraged by Toni's behavior than I was. I thought to myself, *Well, at least I got to use that dildo.*

It had not been love, but it had been liberating. I could see in myself a potential for something more. As the great chanteuse Edith Piaf sang, "*Je ne regrette rien...*"

At around 4:30 in the morning Toni left a tortured message on my answering machine. It began: "I've made a horrible mistake." I didn't answer her; I let the drama and the sex and the heat of her sift through my hands like hot sand. But I never forgot her.

query letter | julia price

It all started (like certain things always do, I guess) with a query letter. Not usually thought of as the sexiest thing in the world, I know, but bear with me.

I used to work as a secretary for a major publishing house, a cog in the machine at this big, faceless company that published everything from literary novels to down-and-dirty men's adventure. I won't tell you which publisher, because that would be revealing too much. Suffice it to say that you've no doubt heard of them; you've no doubt read their books. If you've ever called their editorial offices, you might have even heard my voice.

Two years out of college with a liberal arts degree, I was given the highly skilled task of opening and sorting through the queries sent by hopeful writers. Ninety-eight percent of the query letters and manuscripts sent were wholly inappropriate for my publisher, or just so unremittingly bad that I could reject them on the spot.

Sometimes, though, they're so bad they're fun to read.

This one, the one that started it all, the one that almost got me fired, was different. It wasn't just fun to read, it was a *hoot*.

Dear Editor,
   Please review my enclosed manscript of my novelistic fiction piece *Query Letter*. It's a lesbian erotic thriller in which a young editorial asstant at a major publising compny is entranced by a book proposal for

a lesbian erotic thrller whose authro, unbeknownest to the girl, is a slim, boyish lesbian serial killer with striking red hair and a voracias sexual apptite.

Tempted into request the complete manuscript, she is slowly drawn into a web of seduction by the killlller, who wants to hae sex with her. As she reads manuscript, she realizes that the novel in progress is being written about her.

Soon the hapless seduced damsel with a voluptuous sexy figure and large breasts is the killers hopeless sex slave, pleasured by her full lips and forced to service her enormous clitoris, seduced into lesbian lavage, her only hope to solve the mistery befor it is to late and she becomes the next victim.

Fortunately, I keep a dictionary by my desk; I had to look up "lavage." See what four years at a private college in the liberal arts department will buy you?

The letter was signed "Voracia Lustwitt" and purported to be by a woman. Right.

Normally, like employees at every publishing company, I would pass a gem like this around the office. This time, though, everyone was at lunch and I was sitting at my desk alone, so I flipped through the partial manuscript—about 80 pages of dreck in 10-point Helvetica.

I sat there giggling, enjoying the bad prose and cheesy descriptions, which focused a lot on the shape of the "voluptuous" serial killer's body and the way she'd pick up women and have torrid sex with them. The killing scenes were all "off-camera"—but the sex never was. By the time the guy finally got to chapter 2 and the description of the poor editorial assistant (creatively named Blossom Fuller), I had given up any hope of a kill scene and was reading faster and faster to find the next paragraph of sex.

When he was describing Blossom Fuller in chapter 2, the

author lingered on a detailed description of how her "voluptuous" body looked and felt in her tight businesslike clothes as she read the book proposal. The author mentioned often how the hapless Blossom was "tempted," "intrigued," and even "excited" by the lesbian scenes in the novel proposal.

It was highly entertaining in its badness, like watching *Valley of the Dolls* with a theater full of screaming queens. Only two problems: one, I was alone, with no one to help me enjoy this truly wretched piece of prose; and two, it was turning me on. As he described the fictional editorial assistant Blossom squirming uncomfortably in her seat, I found myself a squirming a bit too.

Now you know why I'm using a pseudonym for this piece. I mean, sometimes I get turned on by the strangest stuff, but this was *really* out there.

The descriptions of the serial killer's seductions were explicit and involved a lot of kissing, feeling up, and—you guessed it—"lesbian lavage," which meant that the serial killer always got her woman into the shower right after sex so she could stab her with an ice pick. Doing the deed in the shower not only enabled easy cleanup afterwards, it kept the serial killer close to her shower massager—which she put to good use immediately after each killing. As I read, I began to think fondly of my own shower massager.

The guy wasn't just a crappy writer—he was *exceptionally* crappy. I've read submissions that were so incomprehensible, bizarre, and offensive they made my head spin, but this guy was over the top. He even footnoted—that's right, a serial killer novel with footnotes, documenting that the large nipples and large clitoris of our main character "indicated a sociopathic, perhaps homicidal, personality." This was according to academic studies that, it goes without saying, this guy obviously made up.

It's not entirely my fault that my thoughts drifted into my own life when reading this; Alex, after all, has very large nipples, and her clit, at least compared to the other women I've slept with, is *huge*. It stands out full and swollen when she gets turned on. I love the way it feels against my tongue.

As this guy lingered over the intricate description of the shape of the serial killer's oversized clit, I couldn't help but note a similarity to the shape of Alex's. And that *always* turns me on.

The thought of it made my own clit swell and pulse. I just knew if I snuck into the bathroom and felt myself up a little I'd come almost instantly. I'd done it before a couple of times, though always out of sheer boredom, never because of a lesbian shower scene in a bad crime thriller.

But this time the shower scene was doing the trick. Probably at least partially because just last night Alex and I had shared some of the hottest sex in the shower we'd ever had.

And even more coincidentally, as I was rereading for the fourth time the awkward but spirited description of the serial killer's clit rubbing against the doomed woman's soap-slick leg, I was shocked by a familiar voice: "Hi."

My heart stopped; I looked up, and there was Alex. "You scared the shit out of me," I said, catching my breath.

"Sorry. You were really engrossed in what you're reading, I guess. Something good?"

I fixed her with a disapproving stare. "Definitely not."

Alex smiled, which always melts me. She's good-looking in the way that manages to be both pretty and handsome, though she'd probably be offended by the "pretty" part. She has a strong jaw and big shimmering blue eyes. Her shoulders are broad for her size; she's petite, a couple of inches shorter than me. She was wearing a tight black Dickie's pocket tee without a bra, and her large nipples were just visible at the peaks of her small breasts.

As she came around the side of the desk to hug me, I saw that she was wearing her boots—the shin-high zip-up boots I love with her dark blue jeans cuffed toward the top.

I stood up on trembling legs. When she hugged me, I softened against her, sinking into her firm embrace. She kissed me on the lips, just a quick hello. Except that my lips were slightly parted.

"Mmm," she said after my tongue grazed hers. "I like that. Does everyone here know about me?" She gave a nervous glance around.

"Oh, please," I said. "This is homo central. My boss just married her girlfriend of 12 years."

"Cool," said Alex.

She kissed me again, this time her tongue sinking more insistently into my mouth. I felt a surge going through me as she pulled me close and held my body against hers.

"Sorry to drop by without calling," she said. "My cell phone's on the blink. I figured we could go have a picnic lunch."

"There aren't any parks around here," I murmured, distracted by the way she smelled and by the firm image, still burned into my brain, of her hard, full clit pressed against me in the shower.

"Then we'll find a bus shelter somewhere," she smiled.

I was lost, remembering the touch of her tongue on my own clit, the feel of her body naked against mine, soapy and slippery.

"I've got a better idea," I said. "Follow me."

It was a bad idea, I know that. Masturbating in the bathroom is one thing. I think most of us have done it: You get bored, you wank. A simple, common occasion.

But taking your girlfriend into the supply room—that's a different thing entirely.

Alex is pretty adventurous. She's up for anything, really; that's one of the reasons I love her. But this was pushing the boundaries for her. As soon as I closed the door to the cramped supply room, she looked at me quizzically.

"Are you sure you want to do this?" she asked.

"What do you think?" I whispered, and pressed my body to hers.

After that there were no questions.

The door to the supply room doesn't lock. Everyone else was at lunch, sure, but they'd be back soon. We'd have to be quick. I pushed her down on some cases of paper and started working at her belt. I unzipped her boots and pulled off her jeans. She wasn't wearing anything underneath.

She had to suppress a moan when my tongue first touched her huge, swollen clit. She tasted sharp, delicious. I drew my tongue up and down on her, suckling it gently. One of the other things I adore about Alex is that she loves having her clit gently sucked. And when I'm doing it, I always make her come.

I felt her hands run through my long hair, messing up the meticulous job I'd done with the barrettes. I slid my hands up her shirt and felt her nipples, rolling them between my thumbs and forefingers. Alex moaned as I brought her closer. And closer. I felt her thighs tight around my face, her muscles tense as she climbed toward orgasm. Then her thighs relaxed, and she spread them wide, open and vulnerable to me. I could tell she was going to scream; luckily, she maintained a sense of where she was, reached out, found a stack of Post-It notes, and stuffed them in her mouth.

Then, easy as pie, Alex came.

Her whole body grew taut, her back arched, and her naked ass pressed hard against the cardboard boxes. She shuddered under the strokes of my tongue and my fingers, and she sank into rapture as I continued working her clit and her nipples.

A few seconds later, her shaking hand pressed against my forehead and I lifted my face from between her thighs, smiling.

She spit out the cellophane-wrapped block of Post-It notes.

"Your turn," she said.

Alex is smaller than I am, so I didn't fit as well on the makeshift bed of cardboard boxes, but I managed to totter there. As Alex sank down on top of me, I felt her pussy, wet against my thigh. She kissed me, hungrily lapping up the taste of her own sex. Then she slipped my pants and underwear down, and ran her hand between my legs, smoothly pressing two fingers into me as her thumb touched my clit.

I was so wet that her fingers slid right in; my body wrenched with pleasure. Alex has this amazing technique: She fingers me with her index and middle finger, working them in just the right way so that each stroke presses her thumb against my clit.

With her other hand, she worked under my silk blouse and gently caressed my breasts, never missing a stroke into my pussy and onto my clit. I spread my legs and dissolved into the sensations, feeling her body bearing me down against the cardboard boxes.

If I'd been touching myself, I wouldn't have come any faster. Alex knows my body amazingly well. When I came, I didn't bite any Post-It notes; I clamped my teeth down tight, forcing the moan of pleasure deep into my throat. It came out in a strangled sob as I experienced one of the most intense orgasms of my life.

Alex kissed my face gently as I came down from the high peak of orgasm. "I guess you could call this a picnic," she said.

We stood up and slid back into our clothes, doing our best to smooth them down and make it look like they'd suffered only normal workday wear and tear. People had just started coming back from lunch, so I don't think anyone spotted us coming out of the supply room. I made a quick stop in the bathroom to wash my face and fix my makeup. When I returned to my desk, I found Alex sitting on a plastic chair in the waiting area, looking like the cat who ate the canary.

My boss was sitting in her office across from my cubicle.

The door was open. I said hi to her and walked over to Alex.

"So how about that bus-stop picnic?" she said.

"Oh, I think I'd better just eat at my desk," I said. "I've still got a manuscript to get through."

"All right, then," Alex said, and kissed me goodbye.

After she left, I turned and went back to my desk. I put the offending query letter in a bottom drawer and tried not to think about it—until the end of the day, at least.

the checker | anna craig

"I like to be fucked this way," she said, slowly drawing one finger across my open lips. "With intent. In the present moment. Do you think you might like that as well?" she asked, her tone soft and alive, intense. She was staring at me with her deep blue eyes, her pink tongue flicking out to wet her lips. I felt mini orgasms rush through my clit as I stared back at her, almost speechless. This was not what I had expected when I made a quick trip to the brand-new super grocery store to pick up a few more eggs and some oil for an emergency batch of chocolate chip cookies.

I had been waiting in a long line when another check stand opened, the Checker beckoning me over. The second I looked up into her eyes, I knew that, one, she liked pussy; and, two, she liked me. I could tell by the amused little glint in those amazing eyes and the way they traveled down over my loose blouse and tight pants. My sexy bitch pants, I liked to call them. I knew without a doubt they were working their magic tonight.

The Checker had rung me up, bagged me up, then offered to walk my items and me to my car. I took her up on it before someone else noticed that her stand had no one else in line. At my car, she told me that she got off in an hour and could meet me at my house, if I wanted. Did I want? Absolutely. And with a flirtatious wink and nod she jotted down my address and walked confidently back to the store.

So an hour and a half later we stood in my living room.

The Checker—who never told me her name and didn't have a nametag—caressed my lips and told me how she liked to be fucked.

"Take your blouse off," she said, her voice a husky whisper in the still room. "I want to see your breasts. Are you wearing a bra?"

I shook my head, already fumbling with the buttons down the front. My small breasts usually didn't need extra support. Carefully, I removed my blouse, sliding it down my shoulders like I was a stripper trying to please my audience—which, in a sense, I was.

"Good girl," she breathed, those electric-blue eyes fixed on my breasts, my nipples standing at full attention under her scrutiny. "I like my women natural. Will you walk around for me? Just your bare chest and those tight little pants you have on."

"Sure," I said, becoming more aroused at the thought of being such an exhibitionist. My clit was tingling in anticipation, and little ripples of spicy desire were flickering just above my crotch area. I pranced off slowly, throwing her what I hoped were smoldering glances over my shoulder and swaying my ass more than was really necessary. I heard her intake of breath, and I smiled. There's something very powerful in being able to turn on another woman.

"Turn around and come back this way. Slowly," she commanded, and I obeyed, feeling that spot between my legs getting wet and full. I pushed my shoulders back a bit and suggestively ran my tongue over my lips, as she had earlier, while capturing her gaze with mine. She smiled in recognition of my actions. Her hand moved to the front of her jeans, and she gently, almost tenderly began to fondle herself through them. I felt such a thunderbolt shudder its way through my clit and up my body that I was momentarily dizzy.

"All the way over here," she said, indicating a spot immediately in front of her. I lazily continued the rest of the way, trying to mask the desire I felt increase with every step.

"Stop," she said quietly when I was before her, inches away. She reached out her hands to my breasts and cupped them, making me jump at the feel of her cool fingers on my warm flesh. "Let me taste," she whispered, and she bent her head down and circled first one taut nipple, then the other, with her tongue, sucking at them simultaneously with her lips. Swirls of intense pleasure gripped me just from that simple touch and I gasped, which drew a laugh from her.

"I'll make you beg for it before I'm through," she promised. "Now. Let's have you lie down, shall we? Right in the middle of the floor."

As I obeyed, the inane thought that I was glad I had vacuumed earlier ran through my head. The Checker bent down beside me and traced my hipbones through my bitch pants until I was sure a wet patch was seeping through my panties and onto the carpet. I moaned, an involuntary sound, and ground my hips against the air. The Checker laughed.

"All right, let's get those pants off you. They're very nice, you know," she purred. "I'll bet you're either wearing a tiny thong underneath or, better yet, nothing at all. Mmm," she said in a drawl as she pulled my pants over my arched hips. "A little black thong. And silk too. My, what kind of day did you have planned for yourself?"

"Not this," I said. "But I'm not complain—oh, *yes*," I finished in a gasp. She had lowered her head down over my snatch, and her tongue was darting out and touching the damp fabric of my thong. She mumbled something indecipherable against my crotch. I lightly put my hand against her head and pushed it down into me, holding it there for a second. She responded by pushing her tongue under my panties and caressing my bare, hot, swollen lips with it. I almost creamed right then, but she pulled back, a little smile playing at the corners of her mouth.

"Not so fast, greedy."

In moments we were a naked tangle of sweaty limbs rolling around my carpeted living room floor, knocking into the couch, tumbling up against a wall. Her fingers explored every crevice of my body. When one of them, well lubed with my juices, slid into my asshole, I tensed and jumped.

"Relax," she whispered, moving her finger very slowly. "It'll only hurt for a second. Just relax and it'll feel better right away. Relax, beautiful."

Maybe because nobody ever called me beautiful, or because her voice was so soothing, or because that daring little finger was so exciting, I took deep breaths and calmed down, loosening up enough to let her finger slide in all the way so she could gently pump in and out.

"Mmm," she said, running her tongue over my labia lips and licking me. My breath tightened in my chest, and on the exhale I came so unexpectedly, so hard, that I screamed, which I never do during sex. The orgasm rippled its way through my body, exploding out the top of my head. She rode it with me, encouraging me, keeping her lips firmly clamped on my pussy.

When it was done, I lay in a limp flop, heart knocking against my ribs, little lights flashing in front of my eyes. The saucy little Checker barely gave me time to recover, though. She worked her way up my body with little kisses and nibbles, pinching my nipples, eating my earlobe. With her mouth right by my ear, she breathed, "My turn."

She ended up staying at my house for four and a half hours, during which time I explored more ways of having sex than I had up to that point in my life. I came so many times I think I passed out at one point—half on the couch, half off. She made these incredible little sounds when she came, a cross between a yodeling war whoop and a puppy's sleepy whimper.

I still go to that store once a week, always at the end of the Checker's shift. I found out her name is Camille. She quietly follows me home, a devilish little glint to her smile, hips swaying beneath that ridiculous red store apron she wears.

I am definitely a satisfied shopper.

jaws | abbe ireland

Rumor had it this girl would rev then ride him with such voracious heat that every drop of body fluid got burned away, leaving Mr. Lucky outside somewhere in the middle of the night, hat in hand, pants to ankles, sucked, sated, dazed, and bewildered with the vague, unsettling sense of having been raped. And vaguely liking it, wanting even more of the fine Scandinavian export of free love: Elin Nordmann.

Fortunately, I cut my hair short that summer. A bulky blue chamois shirt covered my tall slim frame as I leaned against the bar ordering my summer drink: tequila boilermaker. She thought I was a guy. For the likes of Elin Nordmann, I was also pure virgin. At 27.

She was dressed for the happy hour contest: a Daisy Mae right down to the freckled makeup and skintight cutoffs, frayed edges tickling soft thigh flesh just below her crack all the way around. I thought the accent British but didn't think Brits behaved like her: brash, loud, theatrical. She invited herself to sit down along with her American friend. Her long-sleeved pink blouse was unbuttoned two up and tied around her waist, revealing the tease of cleavage. Not cheap but not prim either. A floppy straw hat completed the costume.

Was I going to the contest? No. Too bad. Large eyes behind unpolarized Foster Grants flashed at me under a Cinzano umbrella. Sex in ocular Morse code. But I already had plans to go dancing at Sassafras, the local disco. So maybe we'd meet later. Maybe, if she came looking. Of course she did. Guy or girl, didn't matter.

After midnight, Sassafras was packed, like every night. Throbbing disco music assaulted my ears while excessive smoke assaulted my nose and lungs, as sweaty, intoxicated onlookers mingled four and five deep around a pillar-enclosed dance floor of wildly gyrating bodies. I was standing with a friend among the throng when she walked in minus the Daisy Mae outfit. Tight jeans and tan riding boots had replaced the cutoffs. We greeted like long lost friends. Hugged. I even kissed her cheek, an unusually loose move for me, but I was crocked like everyone else.

"How was the costume contest?"

"Rather silly, you know, but fun. I didn't win a prize but two-for-one drinks made up for it. Are you dating?" She motioned to my friend Oren.

"Oren? We're just friends."

We checked out the noisy crowd for people we knew. Her entire body pressed full-length along my side. Uh-huh, I smiled to myself. Oren returned with drinks for everyone. We shouted more inane conversation then gave up. It was too loud and not the least bit interesting. She finally wandered off to dance, her scent lingering on my shoulder when I turned my head. I'd been marked. I knew it and smiled again.

I didn't make it until closing at 4 A.M. Elin suddenly materialized as Oren and I headed out the door, drawing me aside.

"Tomorrow's Sunday," she said. "You wouldn't by chance enjoy tea in the afternoon, would you?"

Someone else must've thought she was British.

"The movie *Jaws* is playing on TV. Have you seen it lately?"

"No, and sure, thank you. Sounds like fun," I said, getting directions to her apartment, thinking she didn't really mean tea.

But she did: cups and saucers spread across a mahogany butler's table, Earl Grey steeping in a china pot, steaming fresh-baked scones wrapped in a clean towel, butter and raspberry jam. We sat on the couch, side by side.

"Sorry, my furniture hasn't arrived yet from Norway. I got this old Adirondack thing from housekeeping. It's been in a storage attic. Do you mind?"

"No, of course not."

"My father packed everything in crates. He likes making things fit tight. He's an engineer."

"How long does it take? Shipping by sea?"

"Too long, I'm afraid. By the time it arrives, my brass bed will need polishing."

We sipped hot tea and ate buttery jam scones while chatting about life particulars. All very proper. She was more sedate than the day before, wearing Chinese slippers, a long loose skirt—black with a colored crayon motif—and a white silk blouse showing no cleavage but two plug-hard nipples unfettered by a bra. Whenever she moved, she glided, tall and majestic, full skirt swishing, accentuating a thin waist. One leg periodically pressed my thigh as we talked; fingers with large silver rings brushed my arm, sending delicate shivers down my body. Uh-huh, I smiled again. Tea indeed.

I helped clear the table. She pulled out wine goblets and a bottle of burgundy for movie watching, then wheeled a small TV from the bedroom and flicked it on. We returned to the couch, thighs touching again, smiling, joking through commercials.

I asked to use the restroom. Washing my hands, I checked my grinning appearance in the mirror and opened the door.

There she stood, totally naked, one hand high on the doorjamb, the other on her hip. "What the hell took you so long?" she demanded, grinning, white teeth gleaming.

Startled, my eyes bugged and my jaw dropped. So much for prim and proper. Her large hazel eyes sparkled sexy glee as she moved to take full advantage of my temporary paralysis.

I barely breathed as she spun me around and backed me into the bedroom. I was dazzled. My crotch ached. Heart pounding in time to the Jaws soundtrack reverberating in the living room, I was attacked. She sucked, licked, bit, nibbled, and talked with dirty urgency in a hot unfamiliar accent. Fierce. Ravenous.

I splayed my legs wide, ready for anything.

"Can I suck you off?" she asked me.

Yeah. Sure. Suck it off. Send me to the moon! One finger tickled my asshole; her thumb plunged inside my cunt as she continued to lick. I came. She conquered. I came again. Squirming with delight, I backstroked across the bed to catch my breath. A great white predator, she grinned and crawled after me. The soundtrack kept perfect time. It was the most fun I ever had watching a movie, caught in a riptide of play and passion.

We continued through the rest of the film. I flipped her on her back. She spread her legs. I tongue-teased her swollen clit and returned the sucking favor, plunging fingers deep inside her juicy slit. She bucked, scissored and came. She pushed my face hard into her soaked crotch and ordered, "Don't snack. Eat!"

I did. I devoured. My squirming prey came again. The marathon continued past dark, past ending credits until we both collapsed in a sweaty, musky heap on shipwrecked bedding strewn everywhere. I'd never experienced sex as a giddy sport before. It was stunning and addictive. We rolled the TV back to the bedroom and grabbed wine, cheese, and crackers. We snacked and rested then started all over again, making our own soundtrack of bait and catch until timbers of the old lakeside cottage shivered.

I learned more in one night than I'd learned in all previous years combined. I even got to stay over. Guys in town gave me the hairy eyeball afterward, cursing softly under their breaths.

To this day, *Jaws* is an all-time favorite movie memory, and Elin Nordmann my favorite shark.

the puppy, the bondage bench, and me | rachel kramer bussel

A "puppy" is someone whose scene identity is a puppy, meaning that she enjoys being treated like a puppy—doted on as well as beaten in role. She can often be found crawling on the floor, licking and slobbering on pretty girls, bounding around with all the youthful excitement of a puppy.

One night at my monthly play party, I noticed her. There was something that drew me over—that cute face with the big, round, eager eyes, the body shy and small and eager to take my bags and get me a drink. There was an instant attraction between us, an intense spark that saw beyond our natures as submissives.

At that first party all we did was talk, much of it while Puppy was tied up and covered in thick black leather, hanging in a swing after a severe beating. She could see me, and I could see part of her. We whispered to each other in the darkness. "I like you, Rachel," she said, and my heart melted. I wanted to eat her up, in that way I get around true puppies, or babies. I watched her sleep a bit that night, curled into a blanket on the ground, shaggy hair flopping down onto her face.

I couldn't stop thinking about her after that, and we began e-mailing each other sexy messages. We flirted, and it was clear we liked each other, but what could two naughty, submissive bottoms do together to get off? Plus, every time I saw her she was with someone else, and I didn't know what to expect. Sometimes I'm bold around people I'm attracted to, but other times my lust has an opposite effect and I draw back, afraid and uncertain.

Luckily for me, a magical opportunity fell into my lap. We were at another women's play party, which was pretty small, late on a Friday night. I was having an interesting conversation with a friend since I was tired and didn't plan on playing that night. Another woman asked if I'd work the door, and I obliged. No sooner had I sat down than one of my friends came into the hallway with a mischievous look on her face. "We need a submissive as part of a scene. Rachel, are you interested?"

I looked back at her curiously, waiting for further details. "What would I have to do?"

"Nothing, nothing at all." And with that the mischievous look went into full effect. "And it's with the Puppy."

Well, that sealed it. My energy renewed, I abandoned my door duties to another partygoer and followed her into the room. The Mistress in charge told me to lie down on what looked like a weight bench. I was nervous and didn't quite understand her instructions, having to move a few times before I could figure out that she wanted me to lie down on my back, lengthwise along the bench. Then the Puppy was placed on top of me; our wrists and ankles were bound together. I wouldn't have known it was the Puppy if I hadn't been told; she was completely covered, as she'd been that first night, in what seemed like leather, with a hood over her face. The only skin I could see was her lips, a bright pink color against the black fabric of the hood. We were pressed tightly against each other, but there was a little room to wiggle. I started to laugh, and was glad this was acceptable.

As soon as we'd determined we were all comfortable, the

scene began. Apparently, they had already worked up a rhythm, because I felt the Mistress pound the Puppy's back with something strong and forceful. I felt the blow too, though cushioned through Puppy's body. I couldn't see what was hitting Puppy from my angle, but it didn't matter, since I could certainly feel it. I didn't want to be blindfolded, but I closed my eyes anyway and held tightly to Puppy's hands, locked in bondage with mine. She squirmed and screamed and moaned, in that delicious mixture of pain, pleasure, and sexual excitement. As she thrashed, I felt something hard between her legs press against me, making me wet every time she jostled her hips against mine. I looked up and saw my two friends standing over us, floating around like S/M angels as the Mistress continued her torture.

And then a cute little pink tongue darted out of the mask. I had no idea that she could do that! It was quite surreal, in a fun way, to see a tiny tongue sticking out of this black-clad creature. We tongued for a while, since full kissing was out of the question as most of her lips were concealed by the mask. But only being able to touch skin-to-skin at our hands and tongue made it even hotter; we had to find ways to transmit the sensations we wanted.

Her hips and cock pressed into me with every move her body made. I shuddered as the hardest hits stroked her back; I couldn't see the person hitting, but my body took in every blow as if they were landing directly on me. I imagined how it felt for the Puppy and squeezed her hands to me, nuzzling my face into her shoulder and kissing her arms.

Then we became the center of attention for a little while. "I want to fuck!" the Puppy exclaimed enthusiastically, and her beatings stopped as she was encouraged to pound against me as best she could with our clothes on.

We had to squirm quite a bit to get to the good parts, but I finally discovered how to press myself against her to get her cock to slam against me at just the right angle. "Yes, yes,

yes," I said softly, almost to myself before burying my face into her neck, all of a sudden embarrassed at being so vulnerable in front of so many people. She pounded, and inside this heat I came with a struggling moan.

I wanted to rip off all of our bondage and claw at her back with my nails, pushing my hips up to let her cock slide into me. I envisioned the two of us wild and naked and greedy on the floor, no masks and no encumbrances. But that kind of fucking would have to wait for another night.

happy new year | lydia swartz

We smile when we get the party invitations. Daddy and I look at each other, and one of us makes an excuse. So many drunks on the road, I say. We've already made plans, Daddy says. And we have.

We both know where we want to be at midnight 2000, the turn of the millennium. We've planned a private celebration, and I'm getting ready for it.

I cushion and drape the medical table; I screw in the stirrups and pad them. I pull out a drawer, line it with freshly bleached trick towels, then drop in a party pump of water-based lube and an open tub of Crisco. I pull out the step from the stout metal body of the table.

I'm naked except my boxers, except for the bulge in my boxers, except—of course—for the chain locked around my waist, the lock to which only Daddy has the key.

Daddy is wearing nothing at all.

I escort Daddy onto her throne. I lift her heels and settle them into the stirrup pads. Spread out, she looks grand. She is my living temple, the source of pleasure and pain and knowledge. I incline my head before the profane mystery of her, preparing myself to fuck her into the next century.

I kick the step back into the table and stand between Daddy's legs, surrounded by her flesh and her smell. I'm in sacred space. Surrounded by a woman's thighs, I approach the hooded, hungry goddess with my offering.

The first offering is my fist in her cunt. For my Daddy, this is warm-up.

I tease her by fucking her slowly with my hand.

I enter her. I slide my fingers sideways into her. I bunch my hand into a fist in her and turn it ever so slowly inside her, pivoting on her cervix.

I tweak her clit with the thumb of my other hand while I curve my fist inside her toward me, pressing my knuckles against that springboard of tissue just inside her pubic bone. And then I hang on for the ride as her cunt clenches, her ass flies up, and she roars.

I take my hands away to pull my hefty dick out of my shorts. She gasps at their brief absence, but she knows what is next.

I fuck her with my fat dick, grabbing her thighs to get maximum torque behind my thrusts. She bellows with each vicious poke. I growl and fuck her harder.

"Is that the best you can do, faggot?" she snarls.

So I pull out and punch-fuck her with my fist instead. Yes, that's what she wanted, yes. She roars and grabs hunks of my shoulder flesh and upper arm flesh, tries to rip my flesh off me. It hurts. It feels good. It makes me 100% cat. As a cat, I have no mercy. I fuck her harder yet.

After maybe a half hour of ear-splitting, riotous Daddy cunt orgasms, I pull my hand out of her. I wipe the lube off on one of the trick towels.

Daddy is warming up now.

I check the clock: 11 P.M. Yes, just about right.

I get a big dollop of lube from the pump and I smear it on Daddy's ass. At first I use it as massage lotion. I pull at her asshole, tickle it, rub it.

I'm teasing her and she knows it. But she won't slap me for this—though she might when I start fucking her ass with only two fingers, then three.

I know what she wants. She's more than ready for it. She

presses her ass into my hand as I slide my fingers in and out of her asshole, circling and stretching her sphincter each time I pull my fingers out.

"Please," she says. "Please fuck me. Fuck my ass, please."

I love it when she begs.

I cover the end of the dildo with another big gob of lube and press it against her ass. I slide up and down, not ready to enter, buttering the cloth and towels under her. I enjoy the stickiness, the smell of lube combining with her scent.

But aromatherapy is clearly not Daddy's priority.

"Fuck me, you fag. Come on, fuck me!"

I grab the shaft of my dick and guide the head of it onto her anus, which is quaking with anticipation and anxiety. I don't poke. I press steadily, firmly, relentlessly. Her ass wiggles impatiently. I hold it against her asshole. Harder, leaning into it, not moving. Her asshole begins to open.

Daddy's head arches back, her eyes roll back in her head, she is groaning, gritting her teeth. "Yes!" she grits through her teeth. "Yes, yes, yes…"

When the dildo pops in, she screams.

I resist her ass thrusting against me, I resist my own urge to thrust. I slide in slowly. I stop and let her feel me feeling her, partway in, partway out, almost all the way out…then I thrust hard, as far as the dildo will reach, my belly smacking against her sticky upthrust buttocks.

I bend my knees so the dick is angled just right, and I fuck her steadily, growling. This fag is fucking her Daddy hard. I'll fuck her until she is breathless.

She's far from there yet. She's bellowing, pounding on my shoulders or tits or arms, whatever she can reach. She claws the air, rocks back and forth. She comes so hard, my dick jabs her so hard, she pees on both of us, mixing her warm rich urine smell with the lube, with her come smell and my own arousal.

But this is still warm-up. I pull the hot, wet dick out of her now. Her ass doesn't want to give it up; her sphincter puckers and it jumps out of her with a wet pop.

I push down my shorts, unsnap my harness and pull it off with the dick, toss it all onto the floor. I wipe her ass off with another trick towel. We won't be wanting water-based lube for the rest of tonight's festivities.

It's 11:30 P.M.

Daddy's ass is rosy and open. She is ready. Good.

I scoop a handful of Crisco out of the tub, grease my hands and forearms with it. I scoop out another handful and slap it against her asshole. Daddy squawks, then pushes her ass against me, pushing it around the wad of warming, melting Crisco.

I fill both hands with grease and begin pushing more and more into her, farther and farther, pushing my fingers into her. Daddy likes my left hand better than my right hand tonight. Fine. I'm a good little ambidextrous fagboy.

Eventually, Daddy is greasy and I am fucking her with four fingers, letting the web between my thumb and fingers slam into her ass, pressing my hand into her with the weight of my belly as I rhythmically shove my body against her.

"Fuck me, you faggot. Fuck me, please, please, fuck me. Fuck me, I want your hand in me, please, please, put your fist in me," Daddy is chanting.

I let her beg a little more, even though I know she's ready, even though I'm eager to be inside her.

Neither of us can stand that for long. I pull my hand out. I scoop another big wad of grease out of the tub with my right hand and coat my left hand and arm. Then I tuck my thumb into my left hand as I press it into her ass.

Her ass blooms open around me. I push in to the knuckles and stay there, pressing steadily but not hard enough to hurt much.

"Push it, keep pushing, please fuck me, push it, yes," Daddy moans.

My hand starts to slide in. Her anus is stretching; Daddy is howling, yes, she's screaming. I know it hurts. I know she wants it. The sphincter suddenly is loose enough—and I'm in.

I rest there.

She babbles ecstatically, and her rectum embraces my whole hand, her anus tightening on my wrist. I feel little spasms everywhere, pressing my hand and arm. Daddy grunts, Daddy gasps. I am crooning and growling myself. I hold completely still until I *know* it's time.

I start to turn my hand. The slightest movement of my hand in her ass makes a huge impact, rocking her, sending waves of pleasure everywhere. I slightly pivot my hand and angle my arm so my hand is facing toward her belly, into that sponge of tissue inside her pelvic bone. I'm rewarded with grunts of pleasure. Her hips vibrate, rock. She's trying to swallow me.

I'm already reaching for more grease to smear on my forearm when Daddy begs, "Please come in me deeper, deeper please, deeper, I want you deeper."

I slide into her so slowly that I barely experience it as movement. I feel the changing geography inside her under my fingers, against my knuckles.

I slide forward, in, deeper, I slide incrementally, infinitesimally, until I come to the first curve, where I stay. My third finger just rests on the curve, barely touching it. The rest of my hand and my arm are encased in the warm, sweet, fierce inside of my Daddy.

She isn't yelling now, just breathing, muttering. Daddy's hips no longer rock. Yet inside, Daddy is not still.

Her interior is exploring me. Each ring of the sleeve that encases my arm is individually curious about what is filling it. Touches like tiny fingers count the hairs on my forearm. A whole ring tightens around part of my arm, wrist, or hand, measuring its circumference, testing its proportions.

Each time there is a little movement inside her, Daddy

whimpers. Her eyes are open wide as though she sees a vision.

As I hold the space and fill Daddy, her entire interior contracts and squeezes me powerfully, once, then twice and three times, pushing. I yield until my hand has retreated to just inside her anus, but I won't let my hand out. I press back then. I resist. She bays at moons only she can.

After these paroxysms, her thighs shake, her anus relaxes and the individual rings inside her stroke me—not as explorers now but like old friends affectionately petting me. "Deeper," Daddy begs. "Please go deeper."

I slide to where I was before, my third finger resting on the curve, then I resume the incremental creeping. I let all of my fingers creep upward, around the curve, until all except my thumb are inside the next curve. It is smoother there.

"Just stay there," she breathes. I am doing just that.

When I am inside Daddy, her body knows me and I know her body. I listen to her words and her breathing and her moans, but mostly I converse with the wisdom deep inside her.

Inside the curve, I feel her heart beat as though it was resting in the palm of my hand. Once again, her entire body contracts around me. It wants to devour my arm, to push me out, to pull me in entire, to crush me to powder. She screams and either laughs or sobs, or both, or neither. She doesn't know, any more than I do.

I stay inside her for longer this time than ever before. I go deeper. I spend more time with most of my hand around the first curve.

At midnight, at the turn of the millennium, this is where I am: my faggot arm embedded deep in my Daddy.

At 12:16 A.M. on January 1, 2000, Daddy pushes my fagboy arm out of her with one last, powerful thrust. I climb up on her and we hold each other, grease-bonded, hot, high.

It is going to be a good millennium.

the miracle diet | t.c. gardstein

At the tender age of nine, you distressed your mother when she found a page you had ripped out from one of her magazines and stashed with your Archie comics: a photograph of a topless model doing the backstroke. What you loved about this photo was the way the water, stirred up by model's movements, foamed up around her tits so that only the dark pink nipples were clearly visible. Fortunately, on the flip side of this page, there was a diet listed of the "miracle" type, which guaranteed those who followed it a 10-pound weight loss in as many days. You knew that your mother would be far more upset over your real reason for squirreling this page away, so you explained that you wanted to try this Miracle Diet. You were one of the skinniest girls in your class, and although your mother scolded you for wanting to do such a crazy thing, her relief was palpable.

As you moved into adolescence, your breast development was something you monitored with the utmost scrutiny and pride. You were still thin and quite short, but by the time you hit high school you owned an admirable pair of tits: not too small, not too large, with pale pink areolas and nipples. Although you were far too shy and bookish to be popular, your figure won you attention from the opposite sex. In college, you knew of several girls who were "experimenting" with each other, but you were too intimidated to approach any of them. After taking a social psych course that the students called "nuts and sluts," you rationalized that your breast worship was the result of your not being breast-fed. Yet whether you were out on the street, in class, at the movies or wherever, you took note of attractive females and sometimes wondered what it would be like to sleep with a girl.

Just after your 28th birthday, you responded to an online personals ad posted by a young couple who had been seeing each other for two years and living together for the past six months: They were searching for a woman under the age of 30 to play with. This couple liked what you had to say—you did not pretend to be anything but a neophyte in this area, but you implied that the right couple might open you up, so to speak. The photograph you e-mailed to them also went over well, and after speaking with both of them on the phone, a dinner date was set for the following Saturday. Although you looked forward to meeting Josh, a copy editor at an alternative newspaper that you read every week, you realized that you wanted to meet Lisa, his grad-school girlfriend, even more.

You arrived at Aglio e Olio five minutes early, and as it was a mild spring evening, grabbed a table outside. Just as the plump, bored-looking young waitress dropped menus on your table, Josh and Lisa arrived, smack-dab on time. They greeted you with enthusiasm and sat down across from you. Neither the waitress nor the throngs of passers-by perceived the triangle of sizzling pheromones. Josh ordered a bottle of white wine plus a huge caesar salad to start off with; when the entrées arrived—vitello tonnato for Lisa, pollo piccata for Josh, spaghetti carbonara for you—you all shared the savory dishes with gusto. Throughout the meal, you could not stop staring at Lisa. She was so beautiful, with sleek, shoulder-length hair the same color as the wine, high cheekbones and big blue eyes. She was almost exactly your height and build and, like you, wore hardly any makeup. The three of you debated which subway line was the worst to deal with, and then moved on to a discussion of favorite authors—since you worked in a used bookstore, you got even more reading done than when you were a lit major. Josh and Lisa seemed impressed with your book smarts. So taking a chance, you complimented Lisa on her little black dress. She made a face and said, "It would look much better on you—black washes me out."

"So why do you wear black so much?" Josh asked, helping himself to another piece of her veal.

"It's a city thing," you said before Lisa could respond. You worried that maybe she would get mad at you for being presumptuous, but she smiled, showing off her perfect teeth.

"That's exactly it," she said.

"Anyway, I don't think it washes you out at all," you continued bravely.

"Me neither," declared Josh.

"Oh, what do you know about fashion?" Lisa said. But you noticed she was blushing at the votes of confidence.

Lisa declined to have dessert, so although the cheesecake tempted you, you declared that you were stuffed. While waiting for the check, Josh turned to his girlfriend in disbelief: "You never turn down dessert!"

Lisa shrugged. Was she blushing again, or was it the candlelight? "No one was stopping you from ordering some," she countered. Turning to you, she continued, "Josh has a major sweet tooth." You could readily believe that: Josh was on the chunky side, although he carried the extra weight well because he was tall and had broad shoulders.

Josh and Lisa lived a few blocks east of the restaurant. You walked between them, well aware that they were both checking you out. Their building was a charming brownstone, with their apartment on the second floor. It was a tiny love nest, cluttered with books and plants. You immediately felt at home. Josh busied himself in the kitchenette. "We just got a cappuccino machine," he said. "You'll have some with us, won't you?"

"Sure," you replied. You loved cappuccino.

"C'mon," Lisa said, taking you by the hand and leading you over to their shabby but comfortable green sofa. "We'll let him serve us."

"Sounds good," you said. "I just need to powder my nose." Lisa pointed you in the right direction.

You checked yourself out in the mirror: Your face was flushed, and your eyes were shining like two dark stars. You looked absolutely ready for action. As you were returning to the living room, you overheard Lisa and Josh conversing in hushed, urgent tones. Your first reaction was that you weren't what they wanted; you would spend the rest of the evening alone in your apartment, watching some stupid movie, downhearted. But after eavesdropping for an excruciating few seconds, you relaxed. They were only debating whether they should break out their stash.

"She seems cool," Josh said.

"Yeah, but if I smoked anything now, after the wine and all, I'd be too goofy to deal with this," Lisa said. "You know I've never been with a woman before, and I want her to like me."

"OK, honey, relax, we'll just have the cappuccino."

You waited another minute or two before rejoining them as casually as possible. "Oh, hi there," Josh said. "We were just trying to decide what to put on the stereo. What kind of music do you like?"

"Just about anything but techno and hip-hop," you answered.

"Too bad, that's all we have on tap," Lisa deadpanned. You grinned at her; she really was cute.

"How about some Billie Holiday?" Josh suggested.

"Great," you said. Lisa put on the CD, and then the cappuccino was ready. Josh brought out three foaming cups on a tray and you all arranged yourselves on the sofa, with Lisa sitting in the middle.

It was so pleasant to just sit there with this nice couple,

drinking cappuccino and listening to jazz; you almost didn't care if it went any further. But as soon as the cups were empty, Lisa turned to you and tentatively touched your hair. "Look at those curls," she said to Josh. "Isn't she pretty?"

"She sure is, hon," Josh said. He was watching you both intently.

"So are you," you managed to say to Lisa. You reached out and stroked her hair, so different in color and texture from yours. It was like playing with your Malibu Barbie doll's hair. Then Lisa leaned over and kissed you on the mouth, a quick little kiss, no tongue, but it excited you way beyond what an equally tame kiss from a guy would elicit. You kissed her back. Her lips were so soft, and tasted of raspberries. The next kiss was more passionate, and you dared to slip your tongue in her mouth. She did the same; you inhaled her jasmine perfume. "Wow," you both breathed at the same time. Then you broke apart and both dissolved into nervous laughter.

You glanced past Lisa at Josh, wondering if you should say anything to him. His body really wasn't so bad. He had a gut, but those shoulders were so nice, and you'd always liked guys with dark hair and hazel eyes. He was smiling at you as if he could read your mind. Lisa leaned over again and whispered in your ear, "He's fantastic in bed, you know."

"I'm sure he is," you whispered back.

"C'mon, you two, no secrets," Josh said, still smiling.

"Should we move this party into the bedroom?" Lisa queried in a normal tone of voice. "We can all, you know, stretch out more in there than on this little couch."

"Why don't you twist my arm?" you replied.

Josh and Lisa's bedroom was just large enough to contain a queen-size bed, a bureau, and a brass lamp, which Lisa turned on before playfully shoving her boyfriend down on the bed. She kicked off her black pumps and sat next to Josh to remove his shoes and socks. Still standing, you took this as a cue to remove your own shoes and socks.

Josh started to unbutton her dress. Your heart began beating in your pussy when you saw her sheer beige bra. Her breasts were almost exactly the same size and shape as yours. "Hey, cut that out," she said, swatting Josh's hand away. "You haven't even kissed our date yet."

"Oh, that's OK," you said. "I don't mind watching."

"What a good sport," Josh said. "But you know, Lisa's right. I don't know where my manners are tonight." He got up from the bed and in two steps crossed the room to the bureau, which you were leaning against. He cupped your chin with one hand, put the other on your waist, and gave you a long, leisurely kiss. He tasted and smelled pleasantly spicy. You placed your hands on his shoulders and gave them a little squeeze. Then he gallantly escorted you to the bed. "Why don't you two undress each other?" he suggested, stretching out comfortably.

You had no idea how you were going to manage such a thing if your hands were trembling, but somehow you finished unbuttoning Lisa's little black dress and lifted it gently over her head. Then she unbuttoned your paisley shirt and gazed at your tits, encased in your sexiest black bra. "Looks good, you two," Josh said. He had taken it upon himself to remove his own shirt and was now unzipping his Levi's to reveal pale blue boxer shorts. You eased Lisa's panty hose down carefully, not wanting to rip them. Then she removed your black stretch trousers.

Lisa's pubic hair confirmed that she was a natural blond. You were relieved to see she didn't shave it, because you hadn't trimmed your own dark triangle. "You are so sexy," she told you.

"OK. OK." Josh smiled. "So which one of you is going to finish undressing me?"

"I've done it a thousand times, so I think our date should do the honors," Lisa said.

You were still nervous, but when you pulled down Josh's

boxers your pussy twinged again. His erect cock was so long and thick. "Do you like it?" he was asking you.

"Well, we haven't been formally introduced yet," you said.

He took your hand and placed it on his cock. "I don't have a name for it, but we've been partners for the past 27 years," he said.

You gave his cock a friendly tug, as if you were shaking his hand. "Howdy, pardner."

He smiled over at Lisa. "Didn't I tell you she was the perfect one for us to play with?"

"No, I was the one who told you so," Lisa said, winking at you. You felt yourself blushing all over again. This was just too much. You decided that you must be dreaming. While still holding onto Josh's cock, you reached over with your other hand to finally caress Lisa's tits. Her fair skin was so smooth. You dared to roll her little pink nipples between your thumb and index fingers. This made her breathe faster, which made you even more excited. Then she was kissing you again. You let go of her boyfriend's cock to give yourself fully over to the sensation. You were both lying on your sides, facing each other. After a minute or two, she moved from your mouth to your neck, and then down to your tits. You let one hand wander down between her thighs. Her pubic hair was so soft, and her pussy was so warm and moist. With one finger you gently rubbed her clit to the rhythm of her sucking on your nipples. "Oh, my God, that feels so good," she murmured. "Please don't stop…" You had no intention of stopping.

Still playing with Lisa, you rolled onto your back, and then Josh was massaging your own swollen clit. "Do you have any idea how hot this is getting me?" he said. "If you two don't stop being so sexy, I'm gonna explode, or implode…"

"Too bad," Lisa said. "Because *now* I'm feeling hungry for some dessert."

"Me too," you agreed.

"Oh, my God…" Josh groaned. He stopped teasing your clit and sat on the edge of the bed to watch you and his beautiful girlfriend.

"Have you ever tasted a woman before?" she whispered to you.

"No, have you?" you whispered back, although you knew what her answer would be.

"You're the first woman I've ever kissed," she replied.

"Ditto," you laughed. "I meant what I said in my response to your ad."

"So we're each other's first," she said, kissing your neck. "I thought it was too good to be true."

Lisa slid down on the bed. Her breath felt cool on your heated skin. First she kissed your inner thighs, then she tentatively licked your clit. After a few seconds, she backed off. "Does that feel good? Am I doing it right?"

"You're doing just fine," you assured her. You spread your legs wider. With more confidence this time, Lisa ran her tongue over your clit in a circular motion, then over your pussy lips. To have this gorgeous creature's face between your thighs was amazing. You looked over at Josh. His face was red and shone with perspiration. His cock was also red, and so hard, yet he was not touching himself, probably because he really was afraid of coming too soon. As for you, although you were enjoying the experience, you were still a bit too self-conscious to surrender completely. You decide to flip Lisa.

Although this was the first time you had ever eaten a woman's pussy, you had tasted your own juices on numerous occasions, so were not surprised by how Lisa tasted. You had the strangest sensation that you were getting it on with yourself. Within minutes you felt her pussy walls contract, then she suddenly arched her slender back and cried out.

Both of you slowly sat up, then sank against the pillows piled up at the head of the bed. Neither of you could stop looking at the other and laughing as if the two of you had just pulled off the funniest prank ever conceived in the history of the universe. "Is it all right if I join in now?" Josh asked, which gave you another jolt of surprise: You had completely forgotten he was there.

"Well, sweetie..." Lisa trailed off, still looking at you intently. But you turned away, pretending to be absorbed in the books and magazines littering the floor near the bed. You couldn't look at Lisa because you were afraid of betraying your true desire, which was to leave her boyfriend out of it. Lisa was the one you really wanted, the reason you answered their ad. You could have kicked yourself for being so nervous while Lisa was taking care of you. Now her boyfriend was going to fuck you and you were probably going to come but it wasn't going to be the same; it was going to be something you did and felt hundreds of times before. It was easy but empty. You glanced at Josh for a fraction of a second, just long enough to witness the *what's wrong with this picture?* expression on his face as well as his cock, which was now pale pink and limp.

"The thing is," Lisa continued, "our date here just gave me the greatest orgasm I've ever gotten from oral sex, and I...well...want to return the favor. It should be from me." She draped her arm around your shoulders, pulling you ever so slightly closer to her and away from Josh.

You were definitely dreaming. Josh stood up slowly. You forced yourself to look at him. On the off chance that this was reality, if he was going to kick you out, you had to make eye contact so that he would know he was dealing with a real person. Instead, he smiled. "Yeah, that's what I figured was going to happen with you two." He bent down to retrieve his clothes.

"Oh, Josh, you don't have to leave," Lisa said, her voice dripping with guilt. "Please stay and, you know, watch. You liked watching us before, didn't you?"

"Yes, but now I'm going to go out for a banana split." He smiled.

"Sweetie, I said you don't have to go."

Josh turned to Lisa and his smile changed once again. Now it was an "I love you so much I could strangle you" kind of smile. "I have a sweet tooth, remember? It's about a 10-minute walk to Iggy's. There'll probably be a line since it's such a nice spring evening, but you know I'm a fast eater."

"Tell me about it," Lisa whispered in your ear. You giggled.

Josh chose to ignore this exchange with the patience of a veteran substitute teacher. "This means, honey, that you have approximately 30 to 40 minutes to make our date as happy as she made you tonight. Suddenly it occurred to you that not only was Josh jealous of you, but of his girlfriend as well. You figured that with such complex competition issues, you should kick yourself out. You were the one who should stroll over to Iggy's. Sex should not be a contest. You felt noble, of truly fine character upon reaching this decision, and then you realized that you were alone in the bedroom with Lisa. You heard the front door open, then close, and a sliding sound you identified as Josh double-locking the door.

"He looks out for you, doesn't he?" you asked, toying with a lock of Lisa's silky hair.

"Yes, he does. I look out for him too, though. So what about you?"

"I look after myself, I guess."

"So that means you know what you want?"

"Most of the time."

"And what do you want right now?" Lisa bumped her perfect knees against yours. "Hmm…" she questioned again. But you couldn't answer since she had covered your mouth with hers. Besides, with only 32 minutes, no sense wasting time talking.

molly malone's | harriet scott

Just off the red-light district of Amsterdam, in Oudezijds Kolk, there's an Irish pub called Molly Malone's, and in Molly Malone's there is a beautiful barmaid with a dazzling smile. And the barmaid is called Marie. I fell in love with Marie.

I'll never forget the first time I saw her. I'd been traipsing around Amsterdam all day, being a tourist, seeing the sights, dodging the bicycles; my feet were sore, my mouth was dry. What I really, really wanted was a long, cold drink.

I spotted Molly Malone's as I wandered the back streets in search of my hotel, which I seemed to have mislaid; the prospect of a chilled, heavy Guinness was too enticing to decline, and with sudden renewed vigor I pushed open the door and entered. The pub was long and dark and smoky, all wood and relics of Ireland, and the air was redolent of wistful repine, that curious hankering at once for a past that never was and a future that will never be. I wasn't sure if it was the place for me. And then I saw Marie.

"Hi," she said, "what can I get you?"

"Half of Guinness," I replied.

"Coming up. Have a seat. I'll bring it over."

She was Irish, and her voice carried a soft, easy lilt, convivial and confident. It was the sort of voice that seduces you, unconsciously sexy, conspiratorial, where the most innocent remark is conveyed with such drama and passion it sounds like a declaration of elicit desire. I took my seat and settled back and watched her pour my drink. Marie, Marie, dazzling Marie.

She had blond hair, fashionably cut, and a high, broad forehead. Her eyes were large and dark and seemed constantly in motion as she glanced effortlessly around the bar, keeping tabs on her customers. A neat nose, sharp and slender, creased down her face, pointing to her mouth, which was wide and open, with full, calmly perfect lips.

She looked over and smiled at me, and instantly I was transfixed. The most beautiful smile in the world, it seemed to me. Perplexingly simple and beguilingly complex, the smile scorched through the room and blazed itself into my mind. And sexy, so sexy. She smiled with her mouth and her eyes and her face, drawing back her lips and showing her snowdrop-white teeth, her eyes dancing, the pupils gleaming, alive. She was full of grace, charming and confident in every way, a mistress surveying her empire and finding it to her liking. And I fell in love with Marie, dazzled.

I knew it immediately. Deep inside, explosions of desire made me flush, my pussy flurried wet and hot. I felt dizzy and light, my body stripped of its corporeal weight and reduced to fluttering sensations. I knew it immediately and felt breathless and afraid. Breathless and afraid. And in love. With Marie.

"There you are," she said, placing the glass in front of me with a flourish and another flash of her inspirational smile. I felt for my purse but she waved it away. "Oh, pay later, no problem."

"Thanks," I said. I looked at my glass and saw she had drawn a beautiful shamrock in the foam. "Very nice. Thank you," I laughed.

"Oh, it's nothing. I do that for everyone."

"Oh," I replied. I must have looked deflated because she peered at my face and laughed.

"Never mind, I'll do you something special next time, maybe. And I don't do *that* for everyone."

"I'll hold you to that."

"Long as you hold me tight. I like a good squeeze."

"Oh, really?" I wasn't sure what to say, to be honest. She was flirting with me and I was enjoying it, but I was also nervous, afraid of misinterpreting her signals or overreacting.

"Oh, sure, I like a big bear hug. Just as long as it's not a bear doing the hugging, know what I mean? So what brings you to Amsterdam? Off to the red-light district?"

"No," I laughed. "Though I quite enjoyed walking through it."

"Oh, yeah, it's good fun, but once you've seen one girl dancing in a red-lit window you've seen 'em all."

"Some of them are very pretty, though."

"Yeah, sure, if you like that sort of thing." I had rather hoped she might, and once more I suspect I let my disappointment show. She laughed again and reached for my hand and stroked it gently with the backs of her fingers. "Now me," she continued, staring into my face, "I prefer things, ah, more *demure*."

And with that she left.

And with that I melted.

I couldn't take my eyes off her. She was in such command of her territory, so confident—majestic, even—in the way she controlled the bar. A friendly word for everyone, a flash of her smile for the fortunate few. She was maybe 5 foot 4, not much more, with a free-flowing elegance; a capriccioso dance behind the bar and round the tables, shimmying, sliding, beautifully upright and perfectly composed. Time passed by and so did my drink, and I scarcely registered either.

I was lost in a daydream, lost in the hope of the love of Marie. But gradually I awoke. Awoke to see her smiling curiously at me, waving ironically, attracting me back to the world of the living. Blushing furiously, I realized I had been caught staring at her and I looked away, but she waved at me again and waggled a half-pint glass in my direction, nodding as she did so at my own, now empty, resting on the table before me. I smiled and nodded, and she began to pour a fresh drink.

"Thought I'd lost you then," she said as she approached a minute later.

"Yes," I replied, laughing. "I was miles away."

"Looked like a nice place, judging by the smile on your face."

"It was," I said. "It was." I looked at my glass and my pulse skipped a beat. This time, engraved with infinite care in the froth of my drink was a delicate heart.

"Just for you."

"Beautiful."

"Yes, you are, aren't you?" And she skipped away.

I was trembling so much I could barely hold my glass, and resting it on the table I lowered my head toward it. The heart lay there proudly and I couldn't bring myself to tip the glass and break it. Instead, puckering my lips, I perched above it and pulled it gently into my mouth. As I looked up, licking my lips, Marie caught my eye and smiled again, dazzling me once more with her jaunty perfection. My senses were overloaded, stomach aflutter and fingers tingling, and deep in my abdomen eddying whorls of constricting pressure were building and budding, growling and growing.

Time marched by. I began to feel hungry and looked through the menu propped up on an adjacent table. Before I had finished reading it she was there, by my side, her notepad open and pen poised theatrically above it. And that smile.

"Would madam like to order?"

"Hmm, yes. I'd like a steak, please. I feel like getting my teeth into some flesh."

"Know what you mean." She was standing close, deliciously close, daringly close, her hips forward, her back straight, breasts large and firm. Sweet, my sweet, my sweet Marie. "That'll be a rare steak, is it?"

"Yes," I replied, surprised. "How did you know that?"

"You look like a rare girl to me." And she was off again. She liked to leave me with a savory comment to digest, that was for sure.

My steak was delicious, but all the time I could think of nothing but Marie, her smile, her laugh, her mouth, her hips swaying and sashaying, just her.

She returned, brisk and bright, to clear away my plate. "Everything OK?"

"Yes, fantastic, thanks. Beautiful."

"Yes, I am, aren't I?"

"What time do you finish?" The words were out before I knew it, as though some internal mechanism prompted me. I think I was as surprised as Marie was.

"Half past 9. Late shift starts then. Why? Want me to show you the sights?"

"No, just you."

She stopped and remained motionless as I held my breath, suddenly fearful I had blown it. She turned away, blanked, misted over, and my heart prepared to tear itself in two. And then she faced me again. And she smiled. Marie smiled, her dazzling smile.

"Just me, then."

And so, half an hour later, we stepped out of Molly Malone's, the beautiful barmaid and me, the dazzling smile and its enraptured amour.

"Where's your hotel?"

"I don't know."

"You don't know?"

"No, I can't find it."

"Hmm, that's not too helpful. Do you know its name?"

"Something about the Devil...Old Nick..."

"Old Nickel?"

"Yes, that's be it."

"Then this way, my sweet." She took my arm and I felt

the delicious, soft down on her skin. I felt her warmth, and I felt her breath, and I wanted the moment to last forever. We weaved through the throng, battling against the rush toward the red-light district.

Reaching my second-floor room, I eased the door shut behind me and turned to face her. She smiled again, this time for my eyes only, but no less brightly, no less carefree.

"Well," she said. "You've got me here. Now what are you going to do?"

And I kissed her. Marie, I kissed. I kissed Marie, and it was delightful, and it was sweet, and it was so, so exciting. Her breath mingled with mine, lip to lip, nose to nose, eye to eye, and we smiled, smiled together and smiled to joy. I ran my hand through her straight, fine hair, caressing her skull, drawing her toward me, resting her brow against mine. Sighing, for an instant I felt drained, that curious, flat, nervous moment when the elation of the chase diminishes and before the excitement of the entanglement has taken hold. And we kissed. Again. Marie and me, Marie and me.

I teased her jumper upward and pulled it over her head, tugging it free of her hands. She shook her head, her hair careening from one side to the other before settling in place once more, only for me to disturb it again by pulling her T-shirt up and clear. And my dazzling barmaid, suddenly coy, stood before me, her beautiful skin pale and creamy and soft as velvet.

"Time you showed some flesh," she said, her voice croaky with nervous tension. I nodded and removed my top and my bra. My breasts were aching, nipples hard in anticipation. When her peachy soft hand slid easily over the mound of my breast and cupped me, I thought I would float into space, thought I would curl up and dissolve into a ball of delight.

I unbuttoned my trousers and, kicking off my shoes, jigged them free followed by my socks. Marie's hands slid up and down my bare arms, as though she were convincing herself I was real, and her face betrayed eager anticipation. I pulled her toward me, meshing my breasts against hers, feeling behind for her bra catch. Unhooking it, I eased the bra off. Her breasts were revealed: magnificent, bold, firm, irresistible. My hand slid toward them, fingers nestling on the proud slopes, edging toward her large and hardened nipple.

I pulled her on to the bed and nestled beside her, face to face and breast to breast. We kissed, caressed, explored. And as my tongue drew shivers from her, we sailed, we flew, we ran, transported, settled on the very peaks of consciousness.

Her lips on mine, like molten ice, like yielding stone, like nothing I had ever known, and tongue, and breath; her fingers stroking, stoking, soaking, drenching me in my own desire, licking like flames of exquisite fire, Marie, Marie, my golden Marie. She felt for my crotch and felt the dampness through my panties, and felt the heat of my cunt, and she pressed hard and long, and stroked. And stroked. And stroked, dear God.

And then she slid my panties down. Her head on my stomach, she drew rambling, lazy routes around my pussy, dragging through the undergrowth, alighting on my lips and sliding, grazing, teasing between them, tickling upwards, up to my clit, encircling it, enraging it, tormenting, baiting, besieging it. My body bucked, my muscles clenching, spasms jerking from deep in my belly and winnowing down my legs and arms. I had to allow her to know the pleasure I was feeling, and I reached toward her, ruffled my fingers against the cotton of her panties, feeling their dampness, their heat.

The most extraordinary sensations were massing in my body, at the tops of my legs and around my crotch and my backside: a feeling of fullness, of tight, raking, clenching anticipation, a sense of imminent explosion. I eased her panties down and slid toward her, stretching my mouth imploringly to her haven, immediately sensing the musky aroma of her arousal. I hovered above her, my eyes taking in every miniscule detail: the pale whispers of hair glistening and glinting at the edge of her mound, the glorious, trim, unaffected triangle of golden down. And I lowered myself toward her.

And I kissed.

And I trailed my tongue, and I flicked it and stroked it and sucked her into me; I sucked her beautiful clit. I sucked it and rolled my tongue around it, feeling Marie tense, her legs go taut, her muscles clench. The tip of my tongue gently probing, trailing around the edge of her nub, flicking quickly across and back, across and back. She stroked my hair and pulled me to her, gripping me tight, directing my tongue, leading the dance, drawing us to our sweet conclusion. Sighing and crying, her hips bucked and she ground herself into me, pelvis undulating urgently. She screamed as her climax burst upon her, rocking and reeling beneath me in an uncontrollable frenzy.

"Jesus," she whispered.

"OK?" I asked as I slid up to her.

"Jesus." Her fingers moved on me again, probing, teasing, drawing me now toward my own climax. Within seconds I felt a surge through the center of my body as I let myself be pulled into orgasm. I held on to her arm with staccato moans until the waves passed over me.

Then I lay beside her, feeling her breath heave in her chest, as the clouds floated through the night into a new morning. We lay there loving each other in this moment, my beautiful barmaid and I.

kids these days | kelly e. griffith

To start, *location*. I live in my university's queer housing project where crazy things happen all the time. Luckily, we're prepared for it. There are safe-sex materials in a jar in the living room, and books, manuals, and videos stacked on the radiator. On some nights, what can be heard through the walls is more exciting than Skinemax.

It's a typical Monday night. Eleven o'clock rolls around and I start seriously thinking about my homework for the next day. Realizing I have two short papers due on Tuesday only makes me want to procrastinate more, so I go to my computer, open a browser window, and call up my favorite source for online erotica. I slide off my undies and prop one knee up on my desk, pulling two of my favorite toys out of my filing cabinet. I reach a finger inside myself and, realizing that lube is unnecessary tonight, ease my small purple dildo into my vagina. I skim the names of the stories for a title that looks unfamiliar and interesting. I'm already wet and getting impatient so I randomly click on a name and am lucky enough to have found a lesbian tale. As the narrator begins setting up her fantasy for me I switch on my matching purple vibrator and set to work on my clit.

My eyes follow the story. As I start getting more and more into it, my vagina begins to tense, the dildo I placed inside me just moments before begins to glide out as I contract around it. I keep my left hand a few inches from my opening so that each time the dildo protrudes a certain distance I can push it back in. I press the vibrator harder onto my clit; the computer screen blurs as the contractions come faster. It's harder to keep the dildo moving satisfactorily. My body bucks once, hard, and then pauses, relaxes slightly.

Truth be told, I'm frustrated, and asking me to do homework right now is ridiculous. I close the erotica window and open an e-mail screen. This is for my girlfriend. I know she won't get it until she goes to work Tuesday afternoon, but I need to get rid of some of my tension. COMPOSE:

Melissa—Masturbating is getting frustrating for me. I just did and…it was fun but…now that I know what you can make my body do…it wasn't enough. I start to lose control and I can't keep fucking myself. I want you to be here so badly. The feeling of your fingers inside me, your body next to mine; you overwhelm me, intoxicate me, everything. Baby, I want you here, inside me; my clit is still so hard. I want it rough right now. I want fucking. I want hard and dirty. I want to be tied up and fucked from behind with a strap-on, fingers on my clit, teeth anywhere you can get them. I want your fingers inside me, mouth on my clit. I want to make noise for you, and wetness for you. Most of all I just want you. You. You…and then it's your turn.

I'm going to go do my homework now.

Tuesday afternoon rolls around. Melissa and I have a bit of a routine: We have our last class of the day together and then she has work. There's about a half an hour between class ending and when she needs to leave for work. We both have busy schedules so we make windows to see each other. As long as the weather holds we retreat to the university green so that we can snuggle and chat and keep an eye open for the bus that will take her downtown. Today is one of the last warm days of the year.

"Here you go, baby." I toss my bag aside and throw my coat on the grass, gesturing that she should sit down on it.

Her blue eyes grow large, and she jumps up and down,"I'm cold, I'm cold, I'm cold, must keep moving, must keep moving, must keep, must keep, must keep, must keep moving." She's laughing now, shaking her coppery spiked-up hair from side to side with each bounce.

It's clear she's not following me, so I sprawl out on the green fleece, tipping my head up to watch her. She's half running in place with her arms crossed over her small breasts, enjoying the fact that I'm watching her.

Eventually, she collapses beside me onto the blanket and wraps her arms around me. At nearly six feet tall, Melissa has long everything and easily encircles me. My blood is still warm from the frustrating self-love session the night before so I lightly blow into her ear and begin nibbling her neck.

"Well, you've got something on your mind," she says.

"You can check your e-mail at work, right?"

"Yeah, did you send me something?"

"Yes-s-s."

"Is it graphic?" She chuckles, rolls us both over and pulls herself astride my torso, sitting up. She's laughing, but her voice sounds hopeful.

"Not really graphic, but sort of."

Mel flattens herself on top of me, wraps her arms around me, and growls lightly in my ear. Grabbing my earlobe between her teeth she whispers, "What's the matter? Are you sick? Does the doctor have to make a house call this evening?"

"Yes." My eyes light up. "I think it's terminal."

Suddenly she's on her feet and running, "There's my bus. Bye, baby, bye, bye, bye! I like you!" I turn and watch her lope away. She reaches the curb at the exact moment that the bus does, steps up into the doorway of the lumbering vehicle, and is gone.

I wander off across the green in the opposite direction,

heading home. When I swing the living room door open I hear my phone ring. I drop my bag and dash into my room, snatching the phone off the cradle a moment before the answering machine gets it.

"Hello?"

"Hey, woman."

"Hey!" It's Rose, my best friend since freshman year. "What's up, turnip?" I dive into bed with the phone.

"Nuttin'. I just got out of class and I'm headed your way." She's on her cell phone, a new toy; she's likely to talk on it the whole way to my front door. "Wanna go shopping with me for a bit? Tim's birthday is tomorrow and I still haven't finished getting his presents—" bus noises cover her voice for a second, "—portant."

"Oh." I have no idea what she said. "Well, whatever the reason, there's shopping to do. Where are you?"

"About 10 feet from your downstairs door."

"Hang up then."

There's a click and the line goes silent. I drop the phone into its cradle and wander into the living room to gather up the belongings that I threw on the sofa on my way in. I grab my bag, and suddenly Rose is bounding into my living room in typical Rose fashion—with panache. She's a minimalist girl today, silver hoops ducking out from under the edges of her jet-black hair.

"Ray-go?"

"Yep-yep. What's the plan, Stanina?"

"I was thinking the bookstore downtown and maybe the mall for a second."

"Gotcha." I'm rummaging in my bag for my car keys. "Shit, hold on." I jog down the hall into my room and spy them hanging on my wall where I left them.

A few hours later we're sitting on the old wooden floor of the used bookstore laughing about something when I look at the clock. It's 5:50.

"Ooh, I'm going to go surprise Mel. Her store closes in 10 minutes. I bet she'd appreciate a ride home."

"OK. I'll finish up here and meet you outside."

I leave the bookstore and walk across the street to where Mel works. Swinging open the front door, I bound down the stairs two at a time and saunter toward the counter. When she sees me, her eyes light up and she tucks the phone between her ear and shoulder—reaching for me. I grin at her but walk past out of arm's reach, headed toward the book section. The store is empty.

"So, um," she sounds distracted, "the teachers unionized, and it's been really controversial. I can't believe that the administration would be so negative about it, but, uh, a university is a corporation like any other. Listen, someone just came in, we should hang out sometime, but I, um, I, uh, have to go now."

As she hangs the phone up I head for the jewelry counter, smirking. I peer in at the civil union bands and rainbow paraphernalia, pretending to ignore her. She comes out from behind the counter and moves my way eagerly, suddenly pressing herself into my ass, pinning me to the display case. Her lips find my neck, one hand slides under my shirt—pinching my nipple, she breathes into my ear. "I got your e-mail, baby." Her free hand slides down the outside of my pants and is grinding gently into my crotch. "I had to go smoke a cigarette after I finished reading it." She massages my crotch harder now; I moan slightly.

"I'm so wet, Mel. I have been all day."

"Oh, really." She smiles, turning me over in her arms, "Maybe we'll have to do something about that." Her lips are on mine, her tongue hot and sweet in my mouth; she's beginning to slide her hand down my jeans. I spread my stance slightly so she can get in better, aching for her to touch me.

"Please, baby."

My clit is hard and she begins to rub it through the

fabric of my underwear—hard enough that I feel it and gently enough that it's frustrating. As she lingers longer and longer on my clit I feel the fabric getting wet. She edges toward the side where the elastic meets my leg and begins to slip her fingers under the edge of my damp underwear. I widen my legs farther so that she can get in as far as she wants to.

Suddenly, Mel stops. "It's 6 o'clock, time to close shop." She walks away from me, leaving my body cold, swinging her hips over to the cash register to count out her drawer. When she's done we stroll out through the theft detector and up into the street where Rose is waiting, smoking a cigarette. She raises her eyebrows at us but makes no comment as Mel locks the door and we continue down the street toward the mall and the rest of our errands.

We finish our shopping and head home, dropping Rose off on our way back to the residential complexes. Melissa has been massaging my thigh the whole way up the hill; I'm not sure how much more of this I can take.

Car off and doors locked, we head toward my door and she stops, grabbing me and kissing me again. "Gotta go write my French essay, baby." She turns to head in the direction of her dorm.

"No, come and visit me."

"I can't."

"Yes, you can. What about my illness? What about my house call?"

"That's the great thing about house calls. They're always unexpected." She smirks as she says this and nearly skips away.

It's hours later now, close to 1, and I'm up fixing myself a snack. I've done all my homework, showered, and I'm wrapped in my giant fuzzy robe. "So much for house calls," I mumble as I spread raspberry preserves onto a buttered English muffin. The door opens; I still expect

Mel. In walks Heidi, sloppily—she's just come from a sketchy bar in the run-down end of town. Heidi's one of the underclass dykes who lives with us. She's in one of the collegiate lesbian uniforms: spiky blond hair, cargo pants, a polo shirt.

"They served you, Heidi?" I ask, leaning back against the counter and munching my muffin.

"Dude," her eyes are sleepy and she looks surprised to see me, "they served me alcohol and then asked for my I.D. when I bought cigarettes."

"Did you give it to them?"

"I didn't have it. It would have said I'm only 19 anyway."

"Strange."

"Fucking. And then I left."

"What are you up to now?" She's eyeing the muffin in my hand.

"I dunno. Wait, hold on." She looks around the room, spots her lighter on top of the counter, and heads toward the door again. "I'll be back."

I watch the door close behind her and pace around the end of the counter that signals the boundary between the kitchenette and the living room.

The door opens again. I don't turn around. "That was quick."

"Huh?" It's Mel.

"Oh, hey. Here, eat this."

"What is it?"

"You'll like it."

She takes a bite and looks at me funny. "Raspberry?"

"Yep."

"Mmm." In a second the other half of my muffin is gone. "Are you ready for bed, baby?"

"Am I ever." I'm already up off the sofa and walking down the hall toward my bedroom. Knowing that she's right behind me, I swish my hips hard, my robe wagging from side to side. I'm an old-school movie diva. All I need is a cigarette holder.

In my room, I lean back against my bed, letting my robe fall open. She slides the robe down my shoulders and lets it drop to the floor, sucks hard on my neck, leaving a welt, I'm sure.

"I'm so ready for this."

"I am too, mmm, oh." She stops. "Could you refresh me a little on what that e-mail requested?"

I lower my head and look up at her with big eyes, "I don't quite remember, it was something about rough and, um, dirty."

"Oh, yes, I recall. Into bed," she orders lightly. She looks around my room, and I'm pretty sure I know what she's looking for.

"Bandannas? Top drawer."

"No." She looks down, hikes her pants up revealing tube socks. Tube socks are the least sexy thing I can think of, but in this circumstance it can be forgiven. She peels them off. "Arms up." I raise my arms over my head and place my wrists against the hollow metal bed frame that the university has so kindly provided; I know what's coming. In a second my wrists are snugly tied to the bed frame.

"Ooh, you're better than a Boy Scout."

"I've been practicing," she purrs.

I'm completely powerless, exposed. Melissa runs her hands down my naked body once and sits back to look. She's taking her time with me.

"You are so sexy. Almost too beautiful to touch."

I moan, "Don't tell me that. I want you to touch me."

"Mmm, your wish..." she says as she lifts my leg and put my toes in her mouth, runs her tongue under the arch of my foot, and begins kissing my ankle and then calf, "...is my command."

"Oh-h."

Her tongue skims up my leg. She dodges right, slides over my hipbone, and then left again to the line where the hair lightly spiders up my stomach. In a moment her mouth is under the bulge of my breast, her tongue crests the rise and her teeth find my nipple—pinches lightly, then harder. I can't do anything but moan and squirm slightly. She moves on from my nipple, over my breastbone, and locks her mouth around my neck.

"How do you want it, baby?" Her breath is hot in my ear.

"You know how I want it." I ease my legs open as her hands press against my rib cage, ease down over my stomach and toward my pussy; she runs her fingers gently through my curly hair. "Tease me," I breathe.

"I don't know if I want to." She's touching me gently, everywhere. "I don't know if I can." She bites me hard on the neck and begins gently stroking my clit.

"Don't, ooh, tease me, please, please, please."

"Are you sure?" She drags her finger off my.

"OK, don't."

She goes back to my clit, pressing hard into me. Her teeth seek all the soft spaces on my flesh—my shoulder, my breasts, my stomach—leaving teeth marks. Her tongue replaces her finger on my clit and she drives into my opening.

"How does this feel, baby?"

I moan loudly and arch my back as she digs into the spongy, fleshy spaces deep inside of me. She knows where it feels good. She presses her tongue over my clit in circles, and uses her free hand to pin me down as best as she can.

Suddenly the door thuds and then swings open. Outlined in the light from the hallway is Heidi, leaning heavily on the jamb.

"Omigod," she's slurs, "dude, you guys are like, omigod, you're having sex."

Melissa, still with her hand inside me, arches her body to cover as much of my nakedness as possible.

"Heidi!" We respond in unison.

"Omigod, I thought you were making noises on purpose."

"It's 2 in the morning." Melissa is clearly unsure of what to do.

"Heidi, get out," I'm cajoling, familiar with drunken Heidi.

"Wait, you guys said, wait, didn't you say once that I could watch, maybe? Omigod." She plops herself down onto the carpet, "Dude, I'm going to watch."

"Heidi!" Melissa is torn between forcibly moving her and staying put, she's trying to cover as much of my body as possible. I want to tell her that everyone I live with has seen me naked, but I'm laughing too hard. She shifts her weight and I moan, her finger is still firmly on my G spot.

"Omigod, dude, guys, this is so fucking great."

"Why don't you go sit outside the door?"

"No, this is way better. Omigod, are you? You are! You're tied up!"

Mel shifts her weight again and I moan louder. Then she gets an evil look on her face and begins wiggling her fingers slowly. I can't help but moan, and laugh, and moan more.

"Mel! I can't take you seriously with her here."

"Oh, please, guys, no, please, this is so great! This is so awesome!"

The bright crack of the door widens more and an arm reaches through, grabbing Heidi by the collar. Divine intervention. Heidi's being dragged toward the door slowly, not really fighting.

"Heidi. Listen to me," it's the voice of Heidi's room-mate, Fina. "Heidi," she's very firm with her, "take your coat off, take your shoes off, and go lie down. It's bedtime." The door slams and then Fina's voice comes from the other side of the door. "And you two, lock the fucking door." She kicks it once for emphasis, and then I hear her speaking to Heidi again.

Mel, freed from her chore of covering me, rolls to the side and laughs. Then she realizes her hand is still very far into my vagina and it's soaking wet. She resumes pumping into me, and it's not hard to get me back where I left off.

I want to moan, I want to be as loud as I can be, but I know I should keep it down, so I sink my teeth into Mel's shoulder and make small noises. I'm panting now.

She drives into me knowing how much I need this, how much I've wanted this, knowing what she'll get in return.

My back arches and I buck hard, but she knows not to give up. She sits up and presses her thumb into my clit, watching my body writhe beneath her touch.

"Mel, stop, stop, stop, stop, stop."

"Why?"

"It's too intense. Too, too, too intense."

"No."

She digs harder into my clit, making furious circles, and faster into my fleshy insides. I feel it build in me; my whole body is tightening, tensing, squeezing, and then it happens. I orgasm and begin ejaculating. My left hand has come loose and I wrench her hand out of me. She remains sitting where she is as I lay and breathe for a second. Neither of us speak. My breathing starts to return to normal and I notice she hasn't moved.

"What are you doing?" I ask her, laughing.

"Watching you doing what you're doing."

I know what she means—I feel my honey bubbling up out of me. A few minutes later she bends to untie my other wrist.

"My beautiful girl," she whispers, "you have to come look at this, you have to see what you did."

I sit up and she points down. There's a wet spot on my sheets the size of my head.

"I've never seen one that big before."

"Me neither."

She pulls me into her lap and holds all of me. There are several minutes where neither of us moves and neither of us speaks.

"Baby," I whisper into her chest.

"Yeah?"

"You still have your clothes on."

"Yeah."

"Let's take care of that."

affair—in fragments |
s. katherine stewart

By the time she's finished her story, I've finished half the apple.

"But you haven't eaten anything."

"But I have. You were talking."

"I know what I'd like you to eat."

And this flirtation continues, and flirtation after sex is the most haunting of all. She is lovely, tan and lovely and smiling in this yellow kitchen. Those brown eyes, foggy winter forests, stroke everything in their glance—warm, caressing. She stops, mid bite, and smiles disarmingly.

"What is it about you?"

❧

The beginnings of love affairs are like the middles of good books: in medias res, we are absorbed and the conflict is passionate, seemingly unending. Dusty Springfield has yet to sing and life seems gauzy and unreal.

I first fell in love during the Gulf War. When they declared the first bombs over Baghdad had fallen, I was making love on a quilt and spilling violet candle wax onto an ugly carpet. That is my *tableau vivant*, my stained glass window: love in the middle of insanity.

The war always ends. The apple is always eaten. We always fall.

I can't remember how it happened, but I remember our kissing, and her smelling of wine and apples and vaguely of me. What is it about me, after all? She's moaning and I feel her breasts, the nipples hard and pushing themselves into my fingers. They are beautiful. Her naked body against mine is revelation: Gabriel come to earth, Raphael in native majesty—angelic, irresistible. I moan against her mouth, cry her name.

❧

We are caught. I am stiff and mute with horror. My ex, my X, jealous, self-righteous, hypocritical. She called, and she was rebuffed.

I tried not to answer the door but feared the further threat more than the immediate confrontation. I tried to stop her. But how can I stop her—twice my size and outraged—from pushing herself inside the door? How can I prevent her, X, from seeing this lovely *objet desire* flushed and tired in my T-shirt on the couch?

She has decided to make it difficult for us. She wants to shame us. She is a black cross of cancellation to all this delicious lovemaking. X.

Are we ashamed? Are we afraid? We are, just a little. I blush to admit it. We don't sleep well that night. She is worried about vandalism to her car; I am worried about the messages undoubtedly being left on the unplugged phone. I am thinking about restraining orders; she is wondering if I'm worth the drama.

❧

And much later, on the phone, I say, almost laughing, "This was only supposed to be about sex."

Quiet. I hear her shuffling papers on her desk, and there is someone's voice in the background. "We can slow down," she says, calmly.

"Can we?" I'm being foolish. She knows it.

"We can if you want."

"You think you can?"

She's going to call my bluff: "You didn't want this. I know that. You need time to figure things out. And I want you to. If you want to stop seeing each other for a while, I understand."

"I can't stop. You know that." She's won. She's gotten me to say it. This happens every time I try to be flippant and provocative. We both know the game, but I'm beginning to feel outmatched—an emotional position I both crave and feel uncomfortable in.

"I know. I don't want to stop either." She is all gentleness now, her voice feminine and powerful, clasping me invisibly over these frustrating optic fibers.

❧

Why did she say it that night, after the X? Why, half asleep, did she say she was falling in love? I felt a pulling away in my throat and held her, almost desperately.

❧

The day yawns like my tired lover, open in my arms and beautiful. The night before, she had moved against me ceaselessly, an endless current of flesh against my small frame.

At 4 A.M., barely conscious in her dark bedroom, I could not see the soft, wine-colored blond of her hair, but now I may drown in it. Her mouth on mine is an easy ribbon of warmth; her teeth on my neck are tiny spikes of desire; her tongue on my breast is the firm and fragile darkness of angel wings. I can't bear to look at her entering me with long, strong fingers, swift and erect and purposeful. I feel it, feel her. I am beneath her, naked, wanting. She suspends me with her left hand, kissing me, fucking me tenderly, powerfully, and so deeply. And I think unconsciously, my body now an instrument of the fingers inside me, *I love her.* "I love you."

❧

In a land quite distant from this I am the Queen. My pronouncement is: "Words are traitors to reason." I send my heralds out in the cool, breezy morning with news: My subjects shall remain mute until I review each word and pass judgment. Each week a new list of acceptable words will be exhibited on public kiosks. Broken down according to parts of speech, nouns may include for instance: "tangerine," "asphalt," "ghost," "elephant," and of course "Queen." There are certain words I am determined never to accept.

❧

We talk, but don't talk, about what has been said. She makes jokes, having already said the words first herself, and I deny. I'm very good at denying myself many things. She seems to see my hungry look and agrees silently to feed me.

We promise to make pasta together the next weekend.

❧

And now the flurry begins. I am on the road; she is on the road. Time dilates and transforms: How many days until she is here? How many nights will I spend alone? How many with her? I think, as I stand before a classroom of my students, of her body glistening in our morning shower. Her skin and hair perfumed with water; this is a religious experience.

Her skin on my tongue is fluid and soft, the round of her

stomach provocative and Egyptian. I love that she has shaved this last little part—parting, as it were, the waters for my mouth. She is confection and honey and everything sweet and good. I hug her to me, the water cascading; her voice a waterfall of moans.

She can't come. We've made love half the night and it's too much. We laugh as we dry off, and her smile is the gorgeous testament of a love we refuse to admit. I love her body simple and half naked; I love it towel-wrapped and unconscious. She is unconsciously beautiful, unconsciously feminine: a goddess unclad. And I love her obsession with skin care, love her hair spray and eyeliner, love her sorority shirts, and her earnestness. It's all so specific and unexpected. My glance paints her little house with a blessing of love and approval, even the *Executive Female* magazine that lies, somehow unpretentiously, on her coffee table. What have I gotten myself into? Can the heart swell with both affection and misgiving?

❧

I'm Judas. And Peter. Denying her. I keep the sacred secret of her mouth and the religious experience of her eyes in the morning safe in my heart. But it is denial, and she and I know it. She is patient—unfairly so. God should strike me down for denying the only truth I've ever known. I am petty and fear the judicious judgment of my friends and family— they who will say "too soon." "It's so soon," I say. "It's moving so fast," I repeat. "How did this happen?" I ask. And she echoes, my lovely valley, all these fears, perhaps even honestly sharing a few.

But I am a fool for thinking that it *isn't* moving too fast? It has been only weeks and already my mind is tortured: someone wrote her initials into fresh sidewalk cement, a car that looked exactly like hers was parked outside my apartment, phrases from other people remind me of our inside jokes. My mind is under an incantation: *You can't escape her.*

I take one more week to contemplate. I have already fallen, haven't I? It's already over, isn't it?

But it isn't that simple.

With the words unspoken I am still the god of my own universe, I am still prelapsarian, so far as she's concerned. If she does not know I love her, then, technically, I am unfallen.

That's rationalization, of course. I am not ready to feel that aching need for another. I am not ready to be the broken half of a couple, even if she is the other broken half. But I am lying to myself: I am already broken. With the week up, I decide to admit what she's been waiting for so patiently, what she knows is already true.

When it finally comes out, a date I have planned—my birthday, in fact—I've had too much to drink. I did not need the drink to tell her this, not tonight, not any night. And it ruins the effect. And I will never get this moment back. It seems like a bad omen, and perhaps it is. I can tell she is hurt. I promise to make it up to her. But how does one cure history? Especially personal history?

❧

And now the two femmes are making very bad stonebutch jokes: My body is rebelling, and I have an infection. She can't touch me for a week. I feel like a gynecological nightmare, but we are patient, and the jokes help.

"You don't seem like much of a butch to me."

"But I do like to please my femme!"

"Isn't the butch supposed to be taller?" she asks.

Yes, taller than me, anyway, and certainly not nearly a foot shorter than her lover! Oh, well, we make love anyway, '50s style for a while. But this concentration on her is exquisite to me—punishing her skin with my hands and tongue for hours until she is spent, and until I am nearly overwhelmed with how satisfying just this is. *Just like this*, I think, as she holds me tightly, her breath coming in long draughts, our bodies shuddering together from loving effort. And we can now say "I love you" over and over: in, during, before, and after. It is a great, beautiful relief to hear her say it and to say it myself. The hard gem of fidelity in the midst of flowering passion: It is what we offer one another now, panting, still wanting, together in this darkened room.

❧

Though we follow doctor's orders, we are not so good at chastity. I crave her inside me. "Please—"

She turns me over. Her lubricated fingers stroke inside my secret self, the closed, dark part. I am on my knees on the bed, whimpering with pleasure as she penetrates me.

"Do you like this?" she hisses. "Do you like this!"

"Yes! Yes! Harder…"

She drags me from the bed, bending me over the side, pushing my hands down. I am not to touch her. She uses her hips to enter me more fully, more forcefully, pushing deeper with each thrust.

We both know I'll never come like this, but the fierceness of her passion and the shamelessness of my desire is obliterating. She is panting behind me; my face pushes into the bedspread. I feel her in my stomach, in my solar plexus—that concentrated center of awareness. I want her to smash through me, become me. I moan vigorously, begging to be made entirely hers. I need to take her deeper than I ever have with anyone.

Her breath is hot and damp on my back. I am high, lost. My moans come out now as one long sound. I feel heat in my deepest places. We are in a rhythm, a space all our own. She pushes in, and I yield until it feels like we are moving across the water together.

When she and I are exhausted, she finally withdraws. It is as if a part of my self has been taken. During my drive home the next day, I begin to understand the phantom feelings of missing arms and legs, and the difficulty of moving without them.

❧

So here I am again, postlapsarian again, fallen again. I have to face the fact that I don't know how this story will end.

Satan fell only once. I can't make so mythological a claim, though when I see her tonight and our clothes fall to the floor and I fall onto the bed with her rising above me, I feel only the ecstasy of falling.

romancing the byte | kara detters

Some of my friends used to call me an Internet whore—in the most loving way possible, of course. I can't deny the truth in that little nickname. When I first discovered the darn thing in the early '90s, I was fascinated. I could talk to people all over the world! Get information (accurate or not) on just about any subject imaginable! See pictures from countries I'd never visit and of things I'd never, ever do! (The site on the erotic connection between certain elimination functions and physical pleasure comes to mind, for example.) Live a life without having to actually participate in it! The boundaries were seemingly unending.

I remember days when it fell dark and I was shocked, because I'd spent the hours between breakfast and sunset online and hadn't even realized it. Maybe I was a little obsessed. Just a bit. "Imagine—all just little bits and bytes! Numbers encoded into microchips, creating all this! Wow. Amazing, isn't it?" I would say to my friends, and they would look at me closely as they nodded and smiled doubtfully.

Then there were all the dyke sites—I was in paradise. It took a while for my friends to come around, but many of them eventually joined me in charter membership of the Internet Girl Watching Club. Through the years we've checked out sites from our favorite actors (including Gillian Anderson from *The X-Files* and my personal hero, Lucy Lawless from *Xena: Warrior Princess*) to lesbian-specific pages to, once, one of those *Nude! Nude! Nude!* sites. Fun, silly fantasyland.

It was especially great for me because my partner of seven years and I had broken it off in the middle of one of those icky wet Boston summers in 1994, and I was pretty much quietly sulking, nursing my emotional wounds. Translated: I was dating no one, sleeping with no one, and not even flirting. So imagining the perfect life with a wonderful woman online without having to go through the mundane details of real time was the perfect solution for me.

Anyway, things changed a bit in the fall of 1996, when a friend introduced to me to AOL. I was over at her house one afternoon and she asked if she could check her e-mail quickly before we left for a reading at the women's bookstore in Cambridge.

"*You've got mail!*" the computer cheerily intoned, and I was intrigued.

"What the hell is that—your own talking computer?" I asked, edging closer to her desk.

"No, you dork," she laughed. "It's AOL. America Online?" she added at my doubtful expression. "It's the biggest thing since the Internet hit. You have heard of it, *haven't you?*"

Of course I'd heard of it, but I'd never used it. My friend showed me the various chat rooms she frequented, and I was once again hooked by an electronic marvel of the modern age. We ended up missing most of the reading that night because I couldn't be pried away from the rooms full of women merrily discussing everything under the sun with one another.

Believe it or not, that's the night I met Rainsong. And yes, believe it or not, that's her real name, although she goes by Rain for short. Hippie parents. I saw that name in the chat room and was attracted because it seemed like a sweet handle, the sort that belongs to someone who's gentle and perhaps just a bit loopy, which can be appealing under the right circumstances. I had enough time to find out that was her given name and to exchange e-mail addresses before I was dragged out the door by my somewhat impatient friend, who didn't believe in hooking up online—just having a bit of fun.

Two days later, I got an e-mail that said, "It's bright and sunny here in Ft. Lauderdale. But I'm hoping for a little rain in Boston, because then you might be thinking about me. Any chance?"

This was really fun. A woman was flirting with me online from the bottom of the country. No possibility of running into her at a bar, the bookstore, or just around town. Safe, entertaining, no face time involved. Perfect for me in my current state of shying away from physical contact with women. I wrote her right back: "Not only is it raining, there's a rainbow just outside my bedroom window—might that be your doing? :)"

So we began corresponding regularly, sometimes sending up to seven or eight messages a day. I found out all about Rain: her commune-living Japanese-born mother and All-American draft-dodger father (who were now ensconced in a condo in Ft. Lauderdale, happily playing croquet with the neighbors), what it was like being the child of former flower children (my own parents, by contrast, definitely leaned more toward the boomer side of things), her two Dobermans, Gertrude and Alice. Rain in turn learned about my sister in Rio, where she worked as a correspondent for a news agency; my medical billing service that I operated from my home (hence all the hours I was able to spend online), and my best friend Frankie, who was traveling the world that year on the inheritance she received from a great aunt who had died recently.

"What's your favorite color?" would suddenly pop up on my screen in the middle of the afternoon. "Which do you like better, macaroons or rum-raisin drop cookies? Who's your favorite singer of all time? Have you ever been to a womyn's music festival? Did you hear about that queer bar in Germany that was torched the other night? Can you picture raising children in this world?"

During our year e-mailing, I'd managed to turn 30 without the world ending, have a few brief flings, and be the maid of honor at Frankie's wedding to a frighteningly intelligent, beautiful Russian woman she'd met on her round-the-world trip. Rain and I slowly, slowly began to get a little deeper with each other. For my dreaded 30th, she sent me an elegant yet simple necklace made from polished shells and petrified wood she had gathered herself years ago on a Southwest car trip. Hardly a day passed without me putting on that necklace and smiling at it in the mirror.

"I saw baby birds in a nest today as I was walking to class, and I wanted nothing more than to share that moment with you," I sent to her, and it was so true that my heart ached with wanting her to see those tiny little bits of life with me. Or, "There was this stand-up comedian at the bar last night, she was so funny, you would have wet your pants laughing," she flipped back to me late one night when I was up, online, restless from a tiring day working. She proceeded to tell me in detail what the comedian had said, and in no time I was in stitches on my apartment floor, melting away the worries of my day.

Rain had a few flings too, watched her pet-sitting business grow tremendously, buried her mother, and shared the painful or joyful feelings that accompanied each event with me. I literally cried sometimes when I read her e-mails, or laughed out loud.

"I think I know you better than anyone in the world. And I think you know me that way too," she sent one day, just those two lines, and I read them over and over until I could almost hear them in the voice I imagined she possessed. I think that was the turning point for us, when we realized that maybe this online friendship was heading in decidedly more intimate direction.

We always shied away from the subject of meeting each other, despite the great bond we were forging through the phone lines. Until February 2000, when Rain e-mailed: "I have a long vacation due me, and that new assistant I told you about is working out great—I think I'll make him a partner. I'd like to head up north, and I can take off a total of two weeks. Would you be interested in a houseguest?"

I didn't answer her for more than 24 hours, which was unheard of between us. I was terrified. What if our friendship was too good to exist in real time? What if she thought I was unattractive? What if she was a klutz, or hated Boston, or didn't get along with my friends? What if we didn't like each other as much as we seemed to? Most frightening of all: It was clear that Rain and I had a connection that went fairly deep. What if we did actually get a spark going, even fell in love? Would I be able to stand the possibility of another long relationship falling to pieces? My former partner and I did not even speak anymore, after seven years of sharing our daily lives together. Rain had become very important to me, and the thought of losing her sent cold shivers down my spine.

But then, as Frankie would say, what the hell did I have to lose except more time? "You've got to stop romancing that computer and start on the real thing," she said to one evening. "Get with the program and go for it!" *Go for it, girl*, I mentally prepped myself the rest of the night, and it was with shaking fingers that I typed back the next day: "Sounds great."

In a flurry of e-mails, we made flight arrangements and plans for excursions to notable landmarks and short trips to the country. She would arrive in June, just after I finished my last finals and handed in my master's thesis and, hopefully, secured a fall teaching job somewhere in the city.

The day Rain's flight came in, I was a bundle of nerves as I took the T to the airport. Just dressing that morning had taken an hour—and that was with the first encouraging, then exasperated, support of Frankie. "Just wear something that looks like you, and go get her already!"

So I ended up in my standard wrap-around skirt in colorful designs, a clingy but not tight silk top, and slip-on shoes. The birthday necklace adorned my neck, and tiny silver womyn symbols were set in my ears. With this and my fluttering stomach, I waited anxiously at the gate for the arrival of her plane.

We had decided not to send each other pictures of ourselves, opting instead to play the *I can guess who you are* game. Rain said simply in her last e-mail: "Kara, I would know you anywhere." All I knew was that she had dark hair and it was cropped above her ears. She knew that my eyes were light blue and I was on the short side. Breathlessly, I waited as the passengers began flooding off the plane into the arms of happy greeters.

When Rain came down the walkway, I instantly recognized her. There was an air of quiet appreciation about her that I had gleaned from our many e-mails over the years. Her hair was a soft brownish-black that gleamed in the sterile lights of the terminal, brushed back from her solemn face. She was dressed casually in black jeans and a white button-down shirt, well-worn Birkenstocks on her feet reminding me of her hippie childhood. As I stood somewhat in the back of the crush of waiting people, her eyes found and settled on me. We shared a long moment of contact as she drew closer and closer. When she stood right before me, she merely said, "Kara. You're wearing the necklace."

"Hi," I said rather awkwardly. We stared at each for another infinite space of time, and my body felt lightly shivery, tingly. Then her face broke into a smile the most beautiful one I had ever seen.

"How wonderful to finally meet you in person," she said, stepping forward to embrace me in strong, Florida-tanned arms. I felt a thrill in my body as she hugged me, and from the pause before she let me go I knew she felt it too.

When we got to my little place I ushered her in as if offering her the presidential suite at a fancy hotel. I felt jumpy while I watched her dark eyes take in the plants, the computer and billing documents set up in a corner of the living room, the large bed in my room covered with an olive green and cream-colored sham my grandmother had given me. Her expression was speculative when she turned back to me; my heart started beating double-time.

"Nice place," she said in an adorable drawl, and my entire body quivered, especially that sweet spot between my legs.

"It's a bit lived in, but I like it," I said, feeling inane the second the words came out of my mouth. "Uh—would you like some tea?"

"I'd love some," she replied with a little grin lifting the corners of her cute lips. When she helped me get the mugs out and boil the water in my small kitchen, our hips bumped, and I felt another flash of pure desire race through me.

We went for a walk that night around Cambridge under trees decorated with tiny white lights, had chocolate-filled croissants in Harvard Square, and browsed in several bookstores nearby. We had already known from our countless e-mails what each other's taste in books was, and when I saw the latest Katherine V. Forrest mystery prominently displayed at New Words, the women's bookstore, I bought it for Rain on a whim as she was looking at another section. When we returned to my apartment after a leisurely stroll that was edged with sexual tension—for me, at least—I pulled the bookstore bag out and presented it to Rain.

"For you. To thank you for coming all this way to see me," I said, feeling shy.

That blazing smile swept across her somewhat serious features. "Kara! One of my favorite authors—thanks."

Her eyes locked with mine and the seriousness came back

to her face again. It seemed like an impulse when she leaned over to kiss me. I still vividly remember that first meeting of our lips: tentative, slightly uncertain, and sweet, with a hint of the passion to come.

As her lips brushed mine, a thrilled race up and down my spine. A spark leapt between my legs and settled there, waiting. The thought of her fingers touching my skin left me shaking. Her kiss deepened, and I leaned into it, tasting her mouth. Her lips felt silky and plush, and I reveled in the sensation. Her tongue pushed gently into my mouth, and I was gripped by a raw longing that made my arms go around her. I felt her hips graze against mine, then press in firmly. My hips suddenly possessed a life of their own and pressed back wildly, gyrating against her. My mouth was eager for her, and when she opened her lips to me, she tasted like that nectar the ancient Greek gods were supposed to drink.

We somehow stumbled to the bedroom and fell to the bed, still entangled in a mess of limbs and undone buttons. I kept thinking, *This is Rain!*, and that thought sent more little shocks of pleasure through my entire body. Her fingers found more of my buttons and zippers to undo.

Rain's skin under my lips and tongue was smooth and salty-sweet; she arched under my ministrations, moaning and uttering little half mewls that only served to further encourage my boldness. When I explored her breasts and nibbled my way down her chest to the little dip just above her pubic hair—which was shaved and looked rather innocent in the dim light of my bedroom—she gasped my name and put her hands on my head, gently pushing it down farther.

Rain's clit and labia swelled under my tongue, and she tasted so incredible. I held her gently and moved slowly, teasing her higher and higher, feeling every shift in her body, knowing her perfectly. My tongue found the slight dip on the tip of her clit and moved gently, slightly up and down until she begged me to press harder.

I knew in the very moment she came—with a little cry and clenched fingers in my hair—I knew I loved her with everything I had. In that moment, I knew this would be only the start of all the most memorable sexual experiences of my life, because they would for now on be with my soul mate.

Rain and I have now been together for two years. We commuted back and forth that first year while I fulfilled my contract to teach at a community college in Boston. Then I moved to Florida and we bought a house together, a first for each of us. The house is full of dogs and books and light and music and friends and love, and it feels like the home I've always been searching for.

Although I still miss my Boston friends, especially Frankie, I have convinced a few of them to visit, and I am making new friends down here. There is a wonderful community college practically on the water where I teach. I am getting tanned like the natives, and Rain sometimes calls me her beach goddess, which always makes me smile. She is still going strong in her pet-sitting service, although her assistant has taken over to such an extent that Rain and I can go on more vacations together.

That old nickname I had from my friends, Internet whore, faded completely away after Rain and I moved in together. Why bother? I ask them. I don't need to be online anymore—I'm living my real-life dream with the woman I love.

driftwood | lyn davis

Took me three weeks and $285.67 in gas, but I'd driven all the way from my old home in the southeast corner of the continent to my new potential home in the northwest corner. On long stretches of road like that, a person is left alone with her thoughts. I tried to keep my mind from wandering to memories of your green eyes and your gorgeous hair cropped in back, curling in front—the way I remembered you when we met at the women's camp last summer.

I knew more than sex was calling me; I hoped you knew it too. And when I finally reached your door, just being there opened something inside me. No matter what happened, something inside me that had been locked for a long, long time was pulling itself open.

We spent the first few weeks getting to know each other better—laughing, taking long walks in the city. We talked about our past, our hopes for the future. You introduced me to your friends. I found a place to live in the neighborhood dyke house and started creating my own life in this new town I thought I might one day call home.

"Let's go to Long Beach," you whispered in my ear. "It's totally magical. We can go away by ourselves, have a good time."

"Sounds great," I replied.

Finding the right place to stay took us a full week. On the daylong drive we stopped several times so I could admire the mountains and the incredible views from the island toward the mainland. Magical.

After we arrived and unpacked the car, we took a long walk on the beach. I stood at the edge of the ocean and let the wind push my hair back until it was straight as the sleeve on a starched dress shirt. Another continent lay on the other side of those massive waves, and I wondered if this cold gray water and log-strewn beach would become familiar, a new spiritual retreat. I was suddenly overcome with joy.

"You're crying," you said, sliding your hand into the crook of my elbow.

"No, it's just the wind," I lied.

"Let's go in and get warm."

When we reached the cabin, I used my shoulder to keep the wind from ripping the door off its hinges. Once safely inside, I grabbed a towel and dried the sea mist from your jacket, your neck, your hair. You pushed me away, laughed, and ordered, "Get in the tub."

I willingly complied.

When I was done bathing, you called to me from the bedroom. I peeked around the corner and saw you standing naked by the bed. The covers were pulled down; you waved your hand toward the pillows. "Get in," you told me, and I did.

You turned away, rummaged a bit in your bag, then turned again toward me. Your hands were full of leather. You stepped into the harness as if what you were doing was nothing, nothing at all, no more consequential than pulling on socks in a January blizzard. The quickness of your hands as they pulled and jerked straps into place fascinated me. You turned; I couldn't see you push the dildo into its harness, but I imagined your tapered hands holding the shaft, working it against yourself so that it nestled into you while allowing the ridges to ride me right.

Before my imagination finished, you turned, grabbed the lube bottle from the bedside table with your right hand, flipped the cap up, and squirted a small stream onto the shaft you were holding in your left hand. Your hands—your small hands, much smaller than mine—rubbed lube over the dildo, swirling up and around the head. My cunt twitched; my chest tightened. I wanted to close my eyes but couldn't.

That man who used to hang out in the park did this—ran his hand over his shaft, swirled the head of his dick. I remember his cock: big, bigger than any I'd ever seen. No matter how tightly he gripped his dick, his fingertips never met his palm as he stroked it.

When I watched him, I was mostly terrified, partly turned on; with you I'm not terrified, just simply and totally turned on. Your hand sliding on that purple dildo was the most erotic thing I'd ever seen.

"I want you inside me. More than I can stand," I gasped.

Preparations done, you smiled at me. I felt only my swiftly beating heart, my wetness. I opened my legs for you, forced myself to make eye contact.

"Fuck me slow and sweet," I told you, the sound of my voice startling me.

You knelt between my legs, looked down, then leaned over. Resting on one elbow, you slid your fingers into my opening and pushed the dildo in ever so slightly. Your eyes asked me to tell you everything I was feeling. *Trust me*, you seemed to be saying, *This will be different, this will be good, you'll like this, just let me do this to you.* Then you slid farther in, slowly, slowly, so slowly that I wanted more, faster, and you knew this. You fucked me until you were completely inside me and I felt your cunt pressing against mine.

As your breasts pushed against mine, my body opened to you. Far away I heard a voice calling your name, making noises only a butch totally giving herself to a femme can make. This voice continued on and on, rising and falling, and only as my sated body crawled back to awareness did I realize the voice was mine. I slowly opened my eyes and found myself lying next to you.

You playfully told me that more than an hour had passed. We dressed, pulled on high boots, and walked out onto Long Beach.

In the silence and peace of the moment, I leaned down and picked up a piece of driftwood, scarred in some other life, newly washed clean by the sea.

first night in munich or, glittery attachments | juanita gonzalez

"Wilkommen am Flughafen München!"

We stepped off the plane after a 12-hour flight from hell—eyes swollen and tongues dry but ready to face and conquer another of the free worlds (as all good Americans desire). Deutschland!

This was my first overseas trip with my new girlfriend Jenny, but so far so good. She meditated and read for eight hours; I drank for four and slept for four. Although our methods were different, we both managed to conquer the worst edges of jet lag.

I had lived in Germany a few years back working as an environmental liaison between Werkauf, a large chain of K-mart-esque stores, and their Indian supplier of camel hair rugs. I love Germany: the land of bratwurst, schnitzel and *beer*! What other place on earth has towns that each brew their own beer? Weizen, Pils—just the feel of the names on my tongue makes me hot! Heaven. I like my beer the way I like my women—slightly bitter. Germany—it was great to be back. Jenny gently nudged me out of my reminiscing and we shuffled off to find our hotel.

For those of you who have never been to Europe, the definition of hotel takes on a whole new meaning. In America you can expect at least one queen-size bed and a TV for $40 at a Super 8 motel. In Germany there is no such thing as a queen-size bed, and more often than not a double bed is two twins pushed together. In another context that thought would have spiritual connotations. In this one it means someone always gets stuck in the crack. But the comforters were fresh down, and the air smelled like flowers and hops, so we were in high spirits as we unpacked.

Jenny and I had been dating for three months—long enough to know what the other liked in her coffee and short enough to still care. One thing about Jenny: I can always count on her feeling frisky at what I consider the oddest times, so I should've realized that lying on the bed in my slightly sweaty, 12-hour-old flannel shirt would cause her to start kissing me and undoing my blouse.

"Have you ever read any of that girl porn stuff?" she asked me.

"Umm... What do you mean exactly?"

"You know, those anthologies where they have different stories about girls and sexual fantasies and whatnot."

"Yeah," I answered, curious as to why she was bringing this up now.

"What do you think of them?"

"Well, quite honestly, half the time I don't know what the hell they're talking about. But that boy porn is hot."

"Oh?" Her hand fell away. *Oops!* Always one to blow an opportunity. The mood skidded to a halt, so I headed to the shower in preparation for our first night on the town, visions of boy porn still dancing in my head.

Munich is in the province of Bavaria, which is my favorite part of Germany. In Bavaria, the houses all have flower boxes outside the windows, the people wear traditional garb like lederhosen, and the countryside looks like a scene from *The Sound of Music*. Of course, the other great thing about Munich is that it has more than 400 breweries within the city limits. Although I like to think of myself as an adventurer, we decided to start the evening out at probably the most touristy brew house of them all: the Hofbrauhaus.

The Hofbrauhaus is a huge hall of heavy wooden picnic tables and benches with an oompah band in the middle for entertainment. The waitresses have Popeye forearms and can carry six very large steins full of the famous Hofbrauhaus beer in each hand. They slap the load down on the table so hard it actually makes the table shake. You wind up losing half the beer to the floor but quickly don't care. They are my idols.

We found a table half occupied with some young Swiss boys, very cute Swiss boys, who immediately offered to buy us a beer. Before long we were drinking beer, getting to know our neighbors. After several hours Jenny and I decided it was time to go, so we said goodbye and left. Before we got out the front door, Stephan, one of the Swiss boys, stopped us.

Stephan was in Germany for a last crazy bash before getting married. He was a young feminine boy with beautiful blue eyes and an irresistible accent. Hmm, I thought, then looked at Jenny for approval. We'd never discussed anything like this, and I really wasn't sure what she would think. She leaned in and kissed me, then Stephan, so I took that as a yes, and off we tripped to his hotel around the corner.

At the hotel I was suddenly nervous, but Jenny seemed to know exactly what she was doing. We started kissing and Stephan disappeared into the bathroom. He came out a few minutes later completely nude and obviously quite happy to see us. Jenny turned her attention to Stephan's not too big (thank God) erection and started rubbing him. The more excited he got the harder she rubbed.

She pushed him down on the bed, then lead me to the top of the bed to lie down. She kissed me deeply and whispered, "Just watch. This is for you." I could hardly breathe. She went back to Stephan and teased the tip of his penis with her tongue. He moaned slightly. Soon she took him fully into her mouth, and I think we were both going to explode. Every time she came up she looked at me; it was as if she was going down on me at the same time.

I touched myself gently with one hand. When I thought I was ready to go, I slowed down, moving in tight circles, waiting for that look to cross Stephan's face. I imagined her taking me into her mouth, thought about her tongue swirling up the underside of my cock. Stephan leaned back, his face tight and red. I increased the pressure on my clit, slightly, very slightly.

I think we came at the same time.

Jenny excused herself; Stephan and I lay on the bed spent. When she returned, she was wearing a strap-on with a glittery dildo! Who was this girl? For three months we'd had great sex, we'd talked about doing different things, but nothing to this extent. I thought it would be my turn this time, but she kissed me again, then told Stephan to roll over. He looked at her, looked at the glitter, and complied.

She pulled out a capsule of lube and handed it to me. I rubbed it on her glittery dildo while we kissed. I continued lubing with one hand while I reached inside her with the other. She was wet and hot. I slid up under the flat plate behind her dildo until I hit her hard spot. Jenny reached behind and grabbed my forearm. I felt her lean into me while I touched her the way I'd just touched myself, only faster. She came instantly with a burst of wetness and a moan; the shaking in her thighs jigged her cock up and down.

I finished with the lube and went back to my spot on the bed, realizing how much I liked being the voyeur. Our show had brought Stephan back to life. Jenny lost no time pushing deep inside him—looking at me the whole time. I spread my legs wide for her. I pushed my fingers deep inside myself while she worked him over. With one final shudder, Stephan's last night in Munich was over, but as he closed the door on his way home, I knew ours had just begun.

cabs and cat chow | kimberly streible

My apartment was eerily quiet. I scooped up the remote from the arm of the couch as I passed through the living room. I poured a glass of white wine and sank into the couch. My cat strolled by, bored and restless. I scrolled through the channels, not really looking for anything in particular. I'd planned on finishing my wine, and going to bed. *Ah-h-h, Saturday night.*

There was a light knock at my door. I picked myself up from the couch, carrying my wine, and peered through the peephole.

There she was: my next-door neighbor, acquaintance, and occasional friend. Her dark hair was pulled behind her ears and held together by a butterfly clasp. We knew each other socially, occasionally speaking in the hall at our respective doorways. I'd been attracted to her in the past but had learned long ago not to cultivate crushes on straight girls.

"Hey," she said, smiling. "I thought I heard you come in."

"Just got home a few minutes ago. Want some wine?" I lifted my glass as if to offer a toast.

"Sure."

I drew another wineglass from the counter and poured the wine slowly.

"So did you have fun tonight?" she asked, holding the glass with two slender fingers.

"Yeah, just my regular Saturday night, lesbians and lots of booze."

She laughed. The bright light of the kitchen shone on her face, igniting her blues eyes like two crystal pools. "I needed some company. I hope you don't mind," she said.

"Not at all."

I poured myself another glass of wine, and we eased into the living room. We sat on the couch and stared at the television in silence. We were looking at a pack of lions lounging in the savanna, staring at the camera with indifference.

"So where's Jay?" I asked.

"He went to Boston to see his brother. I really didn't want to go."

We stared at my cat as he walked around my ankles and then found ourselves staring at one another. She pushed a loose strand of hair behind her ear and rested her arm on the back of the couch.

"Have you ever kissed a guy?" she asked, looking at her glass, which was nearly empty.

"Once." I took the bottle of wine from the coffee table and held it in front of her. She held out her glass with a smile. "In college," I said.

"That's it?" She sipped the wine, looking past the rim of the glass to the bookcase behind me.

"Yep, that's it." The wine was making me feel a bit giddy. "What about you?"

She looked at me, eyes wide and thoughtful.

"Have you ever kissed a woman?" I said, assuming her silence signaled a little clarification.

She looked away, a slight smile appearing on her face as she did. "Not unless you count my mother and sister."

I laughed.

She seemed so incredibly childlike and innocent, her blue eyes jumping from one object to the next, avoiding my gaze. I filled her glass again. She was catching up to me, but I'd had two glasses of rum and coke at the club earlier and my head was spinning like a carousel.

"Well, don't knock it till you've tried it," I said.

She stretched her arm across the couch and I felt her fingers on my hand. My skin tingled and the warmth traveled up my arm.

"I won't," she answered, and her eyes were fixed on our hands. She circled the top of my hand the way she had the wineglass.

My breath caught in my throat and I held it there. I searched for rational thought, but the wine was seeping into my skin, moistening my logic, and numbing my reason. The woman was straight; I could shoot her from a bow and hit a target 100 yards away. Yet there was something else between the warm fuzz brought on by the wine and the cool wet reflection of her eyes. My pulse quickened and my stomach twirled, churning with anticipation. She leaned forward and placed her glass squarely on the coffee table. As she did, I bent over and pressed my lips to hers.

Her lips were warm, wet from the wine. She moved them against mine. She was kissing me back, passionately, curiously. I felt the tip of her tongue on my lips and I played with it. My stomach was spinning, my head as light as air. She pulled the butterfly clip from her hair, and the long strands fell over her shoulders. She leaned back, holding my hand as she did.

"Lie on top of me," she said.

I shot out of my seat as if sparked by an electric shock. I pressed my body against hers. She was so incredibly full and soft. My hands ran along her body carefully and slowly. She moaned lightly in my ear as I snuggled against her neck, tasting her sweet skin.

I don't know how long we lay there. I kissed her eyelids, her ear lobes, carefully tracing her jaw line with my tongue. I ran my fingers playfully through her hair. She hummed and giggled like a child. Suddenly she stopped me, arresting my hand with hers and pushed me forward. I sat up quickly, my mind swirling as I did.

"I should go," she said.

I looked at her and blinked, dumfounded. "Did I do something—?"

"No, no. I just have to get up so early." She rubbed her temples. "And the wine—I just need to lie down."

"I can get you a pillow if you need to rest. Are you OK?"

"Yes, yes. I just need my own bed." She stood, swaying slightly.

I followed her past the kitchen to the front door. She forced a smile and crept across the hall. I stood in the doorway, staring at her door. After several minutes, I stumbled into my bedroom and fell onto the mattress. My mind was racing, bouncing between sublime drunkenness and a replay of the night's events. I slipped under the dark curtain of sleep, aided by the wine and heavy thought. The strange voices from the television, which I had carelessly left on in the living room, mingled with my last thought: *Had it been that much less than she'd expected?*

❧

"So let me get this straight: You were making out on the couch, and she just jumps up and walks out?"

I cradled the phone between my shoulder and cheek as I hopped one-legged into my bedroom closet looking for my elusive left sandal. "Yeah. It was late, and we were having a drink." I retrieved my brown flat sandal from the clothes hamper and slipped it on. "She asked me to get on top of her."

"I like her already," Lynn said.

"Yeah, and then she split."

"She changed her mind. So what?"

I laughed and said, "Maybe I am losing my touch, if I ever had one."

"Don't be ridiculous," Lynn said.

"Maybe I scared her—"

"She's straight. Come on, chalk it up to good experience."

"You think?" I asked, standing just inside my front door, finally complete: light blue blouse, tan khaki shorts, and brown sandals.

"Absolutely," she said. I could hear the light hum of traffic and lazy ticking of a signal indicator.

"God, get off the damn cell phone and drive. I have to go get some food or I'll be eating cat chow for dinner."

"OK, OK. We're meeting at Delta's tonight," she said, and hung up.

❧

Lynn sat across from me twirling her shot glass like a top. Amber was watching the blues singers meander across the tiny stage.

"So you're into blues now?" Lynn asked.

Amber didn't look at her. "Sure. She's kinda cute, don't you think?"

Lynn glanced at the singer standing on the tiny stage in the corner of the bar and smiled. "Sure, if you like big hips."

Amber looked at her. "Maybe I do."

Lynn looked at me. "So let's hear about this neighbor of yours."

"Is this the one we met in front of your building last year?" Amber asked.

"Yeah, but there's not much to tell," I said. "I haven't seen her."

"You guys made out, right?" Amber probed.

Amber knew everything I told Lynn, and I in turn knew everything Amber told Lynn. We understood this.

"We just kissed," I said.

"Is she hot?" Lynn asked.

Amber chuckled. "Yeah, does she have hips? 'Cause if she does, I'm coming over."

Lynn snorted. "Shut up."

I laughed.

Lynn raised an eyebrow. "But she's straight."

"As an arrow," I said.

Lynn shook her head. "Fire, baby doll," she said. "You're playing with fire."

"Fire's hot," Amber said. "I say go for it. If it just turns out to be sex, so what?"

"That singer chick just looked at you," Lynn said. "She checked you out and you missed it."

Amber looked at Lynn and then at the singer, who was waving her hips back and forth like a flag. She looked at me. "Did she?"

I shrugged. "I gotta pee."

I was reaching around to flush when the stall door swung open. Amber squeezed herself into the stall and managed to close the door behind her. If she hadn't been so thin, it would have been impossible.

"Amber, goddamn it," I said. "You scared me."

"What's there to be scared of?"

I stood up, pulling my pants and underwear to my waist. She leaned over and kissed me. I wasn't shocked. We'd done the bathroom-stall thing before. The last time she'd had me standing with my leg propped on the toilet seat, pants around one ankle with her on her knees surprised at my level of arousal. It was completely seedy, I admit, but it *had* felt good. She flicked her tongue gingerly in my mouth. She ran her fingers over my breasts and then pushed her hands into my underwear, reaching between my legs. She pulled back and looked at me.

"What's wrong, cupcake?" she said.

"I think I'm going to call it a night," I said. I didn't feel like getting drunk or fucking around with Amber in the bathroom stall. I really just wanted to go home.

"Does this bother you?" she said, extracting her hand from between my legs.

I shook my head. "Just tired."

She nodded and smiled. "OK. I mean, we could do this at your apartment or possibly mine, but then we'd be dating, wouldn't we? And we can't have that."

I laughed. "No, we can't," I said.

She leaned over and sucked my bottom lip. "Need a ride?"

"No," I said. "I'll catch a cab."

That was my life after all: cabs and cat chow.

❧

My arms began to feel tired and my legs heavy as I climbed the stairs to my apartment; three bags of groceries for four blocks and I was ready to flop into the nearest chair. I needed to rethink my decision to take fewer cab rides. I hooked my hip under a brown bag and squirmed my arm around the bulk, inserting my key haphazardly into the lock.

"Need some help?" she called from behind me.

I turned on my side, careful not to spill the bags. She was wearing a plain white T-shirt and blue jeans, staring at me with her wide blue eyes.

"Sure, if you could grab this one on the outside."

I shoved a bag in her direction; she scooped it from my arms. I pushed open my front door and stumbled in. I placed the two bags onto the kitchen table, and she set the third beside them.

"Thanks," I said.

She leaned languidly in the kitchen entrance as I anxiously began unpacking my groceries. I glanced at her as I pulled the bag of bagels from the paper bag and set them on the counter. Freshly showered: There were small beads of water on her neck. She smelled like cocoa butter.

It suddenly became evident to me, as my pulse quickened and unnerving fragmented thoughts filtered into my brain, that I was more than just mildly attracted to this woman; I struggled with my thoughts, too careful of what to say, too nervous of what not to say. I felt increasingly anxious as she stood quietly in my kitchen, silent but watchful.

"I just wanted to say something about the other night," she said. She placed a hand onto the counter. "I'm really sorry I left like that."

"Me too," I said. I couldn't think of anything better to say. I was chewing my bottom lip.

She motioned toward the front door. "I should get back, then, I guess."

I walked toward the front door to see her out. I didn't have enough time to turn around before I felt her breasts against my back. She wrapped her arms around my waist.

"I'm a little scared," she said. "Is this OK?"

I turned, feeling her hands move against my waist. "Yes," I told her.

She pulled her damp, white T-shirt over her head. She wasn't wearing anything underneath; her breasts stood between us, full and flirtatious. She kissed me again and we stumbled toward the couch, undressing and kissing, touching and tearing at our clothes as if we might suddenly combust.

We rolled around on the couch, swapping positions, exploring, flirting, tasting. Her wet hair against the inside of my thighs sent a penetrating quiver through my legs. I laughed aloud, terribly excited by her sudden abandon of the careful, thoughtful woman I knew. I kissed the inside of her knee and she laughed.

She jumped from the couch and I followed her. We threw ourselves onto my bed, our legs and arms soon entangled. I hadn't had the slightest taste of wine all day, but I felt as if I had, the swirling of my thoughts, fast images not really linking themselves in my mind, just fast and colorful pictures flashing before my eyes like a string of hallucinations.

We rolled together on the bed, twirling my olive-green sheets around us. I circled her nipples with tongue and gently squeezed her breasts. I traced a trail from her breast down her stomach with my tongue. I swirled my tongue around her belly button, slid down the mattress, position myself between her legs, feeling her thighs against my shoulders. She caressed my hair and arched her back. I kissed the inside of her thighs, gripped her soft buttocks with my hands, pushed my tongue between her moist lips, into her warm wetness. She moaned and muttered something inaudible. She pressed her back into the mattress, pushing herself into my face. I moved my tongue in and out, holding the backs of her thighs in my hands.

She took in quick breaths and released them in short, guttural bursts. I moved my tongue inside her, making small circles. I felt her leg muscles tighten, her knees squeezing me tightly. She squirmed beneath me, gripping my hair in her tight fist. She pushed against my shoulders; I sat up looking down at her, amazed by her beauty.

She lay silent for several moments. I stretched my body along hers, resting my head against her shoulder. With her weight resting on her elbow, she leaned over and kissed me long and deep, then swung her legs over my waist and sat on top of me. The heat between her legs mingled with my own. She leaned forward, her breasts brushing against mine, and kissed my forehead and then my eyelids.

She giggled. "I don't know what I'm doing."

I started to reply, but she covered my mouth with hers. She teasingly flicked her tongue along my lips and then along my neck. She squeezed my breasts and began kissing them lightly. I felt a surge of electricity as she sucked and nibbled my nipples. A bolt shot through my spine, hot and intense as she thrust her face between my legs, moving her mouth with great intensity. I tried to fend off the waves building in my stomach and traveling down to my toes. I was a well, drained and replenished. I could hear my own voice: low, deep, indiscernible broken vowels swirling around the room.

I gathered my senses, a sense of normality sweeping over my tingling pores. She snuggled against my side, her fingers drawing circles on my stomach.

"Were you faking?" she said, out of the blue.

I looked at her. Her eyes were warm, wet, inviting. "No."

I brushed a strand of hair from her face. She closed her eyes, and I watched her for a moment. I felt sleep creeping around the edges of my body, seeping, heavy and full. Before sleep there were the images of her: slow movements, soft skin, a warm drink, moist lips.

The afternoon sun crept through the blinds, casting slanted yellow lines across the mattress. My mind began to unwind, shaking the remnants of dream. The air in my bedroom was thick, smelling like sweat and cocoa butter. I sat up, suddenly aware that she was gone. It was 6:30. I was supposed to meet Lynn and Amber at the Delta at 7. I didn't want to go; I wanted to go next door. But what if her husband answered? What would I say? "I fucked your wife this afternoon and was wondering if maybe she wanted to go for a drink."

I crawled into the cab. I couldn't shake the feel of her skin, her moist lips, or the smell of her from my mind. I didn't want to.

Amber and Lynn were waiting and as usual had already had a few drinks. "You're late," Lynn said.

"So sue me," I said.

"I would, but you don't own shit—what would I get?"

I shrugged. "A used dildo and some old paper clippings."

"Gross," Amber said.

We laughed.

Amber finished her drink and sat the glass down heavily on the table.

"Shit," she said. "My panties just slid to the floor, girls."

Lynn looked at the dance floor. There was only one couple, their breasts rubbing and rolling.

"No," Amber said. "Look who just walked in."

I turned and my mouth fell open. She walked across the bar and sat beside me, resting her arm on the back of my chair. Lynn and Amber stared at her with their mouths open. We must have looked like the Three Stooges.

She looked at me and smiled. "Why didn't you let me know you were leaving?" The blue eyes and the cocoa butter were making my stomach twirl. She nudged me with her shoulder. "Let me know next time," she said. "We'll share a cab."

kate, nyc | tara-michelle ziniuk

I'm not from New York City; as far as I can tell no one really is—no one except her. And the way the grips on her boots fit into the grooves on the dance floor you'd think she came with the bar.

She is New York City, the kind of dirty that no shower can fix. A combination of Lynn Breedlove and Trent Reznor, an unpop cultural icon, a macho Lili Taylor. She is repulsive at a glance, stunning at another. She has faded patches down her pant legs, political patches overlapping each other until they are almost illegible. Her body hides behind her clothes, making you wonder if she's wearing the same worn black lace bra she did in high school, torn in all of the right places, or a men's undershirt.

I'm sizing her up from my post by the bar. Cliché of all clichés, I'm trying to plan my next move. Tonight I'm wearing boots that are actually comfortable—they make me walk tough while simultaneously screaming "high-femme princess." I order a vodka cranberry; it matches my lipstick. I want her looking at my lips. As the bartender looks away, I steal a thin red straw and a cherry from the other side of the counter—a straw so as not to mess up the lipstick and the cherry in case she is watching.

I drink enough of my drink to feel it; I've been pacing and move on to a second cocktail. I walk closer to her and lean against a beam. My weight leans into the metal behind me; it is holding up the ceiling, and she is holding up the room. I look hard at her as the band rocks out the last song of their set. She's doing the head-shaking "no one else is in the room" thing. I want to run my hands through her sweaty hair before it dries. I want to stub out her cigarette and taste the smoke off her fingers as I bite them. I lower my eyes, pull my body to a standing position, eat my maraschino cherries, red sex, confidence like blood, and walk over.

Her eyes follow my approach. She greets me with the generic butch-girl chin nod. I'm not sure when she stepped toward me, but that chin is now lingering just over the top of my head. I am staring into her collarbone, unable to make eye contact like this. I'm feeling my bad-girl attitude dissolve into unexpected bashfulness. Her warm hand is suddenly flat against my stomach; it rises and falls with my breathing while her chest remains oddly still.

I was planning on taking charge of this one and am impressed with her having switched the scene before it really began. She moved behind me, hand still firm on my stomach, and is leading me toward the bar, using her free hand to lift a well-worn black leather jacket from one of the barstools, and expertly drapes it over my shoulders. I don't want to ruin our silence, but I'm worried about my coat being left behind. Before I'm able to speak, she brings us to where I'd tossed my coat and now has the faux fur folded over her shoulder. She'd apparently seen me here earlier; I'm pleased with myself for having made myself noticeable and with her for not having let on. Her carrying my coat makes me feel like a bit of a queen—a queen being abducted from a Lower East Side bar by a woman with whom I have yet to exchange a smile, never mind a word. Maybe, I tell myself, this type of thing happens all the time in New York. This is, after all, the city where tough girls are made. Maybe this isn't creepy—maybe it's *authentic*.

She walks us down a series of similar-looking streets, past

a number of all-American concrete parks and little intersections of sidewalks with metal gym structures for children. Long after I've given up trying to remember the street names, we're walking over a highway overpass. She maneuvers me toward the wall of the bridge, facing out over the traffic. The place she's chosen to stop is very desolate and very public—a thoughtful choice; she knows her city. I'm torn between excitement and the instinct to be facing her. She moves her hand steadily along the curve of my hip. Despite the whole kidnapping arrangement I feel protected under the foreign leather and the hands to which it belongs.

I feel her breath against the nape of my neck. She lifts my dress very slowly, allowing the chilled air to draw sensations along the backs of my thighs. She traces her tongue lightly up my legs, taking small bites up my sides until she's again standing behind me, her face pressed against my neck.

When she turns me around, her head is lowered; I still can't meet her eyes. She's in control and strategic. She lifts me up so that I'm sitting on top of the ledge. Looking down on her I felt a new authority, and acting on this impulse immediately I grab the already torn neckline of her shirt and yank her toward me. She pulls back quickly and rolls her face against my chest, biting my nipples through the fabric of my shirt until they are erect. She gently laps her tongue down the seam of my torso, biting at the soft flesh above each hip bone, then moves her hot breath up and down the insides of my thighs.

When she runs her face against the top edge of my boots, I decide this is my chance to cut in and play with the power dynamic. Her eyes aren't even looking at me when I open my mouth, but somehow her fingers find my lips and obstruct any sound from escaping. I suck the salt and nicotine from her fingers. I've never been a smoker, but I have a weakness for rough hands that taste of cigarettes. When I release her hands from my mouth she massages my calves through the stiff boots. She feels them over thoroughly and cautiously before kissing them all over. She tilts her head back and lets me push my soles against her neck one at a time. As she leans further back, I graze my boots over her body, eventually pushing my strength onto the tops of her thighs.

She sits upright, locking her hands behind her back. And for the first time she touches my face with hers. She breathes into my ear, and I finally hear her voice: "Princess," she says, just above a whisper.

I motion with one index finger, and she brings her ear to my lips. My voice is hoarse but clear: "You are very sweet, but you were not asked to speak." She looks up to meet my expression with a new sweetness; she smiles at me.

I take her lower lip into my mouth and bite it, inviting what will be the first kiss with this girl I have been waiting for all night. The kiss is deep and hard. It lasts until I grab the bleached ends of the dark-rooted hair above her neckline and pull her face away. Still holding her there, I stand and realize that in the boots I'm taller than she is.

When I let go of her, I take her in completely; she's the perfect coy punkboi slouching in front of me. This is what draws me to her—that there is personality at play, that she isn't a small soldier waiting for me but someone I'm intrigued to know. She's staring into my chest, shuffling her scuffed boots into the pavement as I pull down the zipper on the side of my dress. I pull her hand toward me and fit it into the new opening of the dress. Her hand is strong and rough as it traces the satin seams of my bra from the back around to the front.

I slip down the straps of the dress and allow her to continue to explore. She lowers the straps of my white-dotted red rockabilly bra and kisses my shoulders. I pick up the pace and dig my nails into the back of her neck as she licks my breasts and bites at their fleshiness. She's rough with my newly sensitive nipples and pulls with her teeth at the tiny silver barbells piercing them. She's sucking at my nipple, pulling up as she raises her head to look at me.

She quickly kisses her way down my torso, and soon her hot mouth is on my cunt through the black lace I am not yet allowing her to remove. I feel her tongue push my own wetness against me. Sexy hands press against my ass. I lean my head down so my hair is tickling the length of her back as I pull her shirt over her head. I bite her neck viciously, pulling at the bike chains she has secured around her neck. When she runs her fingers along the inside of the trim of my panties, I know she's about to try to get under them. This is what I want too, but right now I'm a committed tease getting off on the power of being desired. I pull her hair up from the top now: "Stop." She freezes with one hand still cupped under me.

I move her slowly as not to shift her much wanted hand. When I have her pushed up against the wall I hold her head back, again by the hair, and torture her, tonguing and chewing on her ear. When she starts moaning, I grasp one hand around the chains she wears around her neck. With the other hand I push firmly at the bare skin of her back. Her loose pants give easy access; I slip my hand down the back of her worn gray boxers. I can tell she wants to say something, so I cover her mouth with three harsh fingers, shaking my head in my most disciplinary no-nonsense manner. I take my fingers from her lips and hold them in front of her to be kissed. Once she has done this properly, I undo her belt and force my hand into the fly of her boxers. She leans herself into my hand, and I feel her now-exposed wetness. I move the three fingers that were silencing her to the opening of her cunt and tease her, flickering across the opening. Then I move her hand to her clit. She rubs slowly, biting her lip again.

I start to kiss and fuck her at the same time; her body thrusts. My three fingers move easily in and out of her slippery pussy. I add in the forth and push hard. She's making muffled low sounds that turn me on. The hand she still has under me feels like it's planted there to catch my dripping want for her.

I'm fucking her hard now and she's biting down on my shoulder. When I know she's about to come I pause for a moment and say into her ear, "Louder, and only for me." Her face moves to my ear, and she follows my orders well, moaning loudly into it. The sounds increase. The hand she still has under me squeezes against my ass. Her other hand speeds up as I lean in to fuck her deeper, harder. She comes loudly, her hot breath leaving moisture on my neck. I hold her there with until my fingers feel she has stopped trembling.

I look around the ground for my coat, put it on, hiding my otherwise mostly naked body, and throw her leather over my shoulder. I see on the inside she'd written "Kate" with a sharpie. Then while she's fumbling with her belt I lean my lips into her ear, holding her flushed face in my hand, and whisper, "Thanks, princess."

the ladies get a name | lynn herr

It was the third time in as many years and in as many cities that I'd tried to take a figure painting class, only to be told I had to complete the figure drawing course first. But, I pleaded with my new instructor, I've already taken the figure drawing class in Portland and Boise. Well, she told me, I'm sorry, but you need to take it again. If these classes had been for grades, I could've shown her my transcript, but alas, I had entered the world of adult classes.

So two weeks later I sat down in my stained white overcoat and paint-splattered jeans, a conte stick in one hand and a tall glass of sun tea in the other, waiting for yet another model to spin three-minute poses. The class was almost entirely comprised of women in their early 30s—an odd string I've found in nearly every adult art class I've taken.

Beth, Nicki, Amie, Angela, Catie, our shy boy Mel, and I all poised our conte on our three-foot sheets of scrap paper clipped to our easels and waited. And waited. And waited. Finally the teacher, a long-haired Smurf of a woman wearing a dress of various browns who insisted we call her Peach, moved to the dressing room off to the side. Ordinarily the model emerges from the room, walks to the center of our easel circle, drops his or her robe, then follows the teacher's instructions.

Peach knocked a few times on the door. "Yes? I'm sorry," came the reply. "I mean, I seem to be stuck. Lord knows how...this is really embarrassing."

"Do you need help?" Peach asked in a hushed toned.

"Yeah, that'd be great."

Peach opened the door and after some rustling and a few "ouch"es, she brought out the model du jour: a beautiful woman with messy hair and Urban Decay nail polish. "Hi, everyone—sorry about the delay. I was trying to push a bug through the crack in the side wall when I got my foot stuck. Or, I mean, my boot stuck but it also came with the foot—"

Models are to remain silent during their time in class because teachers want their students to view the model not as a person but as a series of shapes placed together in a pattern. They worry that if we personalize the figure, the objectivity of our drawing may be compromised. As our model rambled on, we each found ourselves charmed and perhaps, in some cases, connected and suddenly awkward at having her shed her clothing. I mean, I hadn't even bought her dinner yet.

Peach made her most aggressive move yet, sliding across the floor in her faux leather sandals and grabbing our model by the arm to move her into position. "Please keep silent," she whispered. The model smiled at Peach who remained unamused, then told her to "hold a standing pose, arm up, for five minutes."

Now, you may not think this sounds difficult, but I can assure you it is. Holding any pose for more than two or three minutes is tough, but holding your arm out for five minutes while standing is grueling. After two minutes your arm shakes, your feet hurt, and you have a tickle on your nose. After four minutes your muscles ache and your hips feel stiff. By five minutes most models are either in the zone and detached from it all, or telling the instructor to screw them-selves as they sail out toward the coffee machine.

Our model did none of these things. Instead, about three minutes into it, she told everyone she needed to rest her arm for 30 seconds. She suggested we take the time to focus on her lower body. Peach was beside herself.

"You need to maintain the pose requested for the time requested," she curtly informed our model.

"Listen," came the response, "I apologize for the talking, but this is killing my arm. I don't see how 30 seconds matters, especially when I'll maintain position for my lower half—agreed?"

We were dumbstruck. Only Beth and Amie continued drawing, determined to maintain objectivity. Meanwhile, I couldn't help wonder why she had about a dozen little footprints tattooed in winding patterns up the back of her right leg.

"I have a pogo game night tonight with some friends, and for $7.50 an hour I can't jeopardize my chance for holding down my title—"

"This is your job," Peach began.

"You're right," the model smiled, knowing full well that their argument had actually gained her an extra 30-second break. "I'm sorry. Let's continue."

After class, I grabbed a cup of cocoa from the machine and waited for her to finish dressing.

"You're definitely the most interesting model I've ever drawn," I told her when she popped out of the drawing room, a huge safari-beige satchel over her shoulder.

"Thanks, I think. Peach is a terror, huh? Uptight."

"This is my first class with her."

"This was my first time modeling ever. What an intro. Jesus."

"I'm Lynn."

"Hey, Lynn. I'm Georgia. Yes, the thing my daddy always had on his mind. Corny, but it was the mid '60s, so they can be forgiven."

Mid '60s, I thought. *She's my age.*

"Yeah, I am kind of old to be working for $7.50 an hour." She must've knew I was calculating her age.

"No—"

"I'm an actor."

Uh-oh, I thought.

"No, No. Not a bad one. I mean, well, you know what I mean. Anyway, I decided to do this so I could get over my fear of being naked in front of people. Not that I have to be naked to act, but it helps that I can be naked without passing out. Then when I'm doing a love scene, it doesn't feel like a big deal. Speaking of boobs, my pogo competition's in two hours, so I have to grab some chow. Build my stamina, you know."

I suggested we stop by the taco stand next door for their cheese enchilada platter and a few *cervezas*. "Nothing," I rationalized to her, "helps pogo balance more than relaxation. And nothing relaxes more than a few *cervezas*."

We talked about our love of old Dinosaur Jr. records, our useless liberal arts degrees, ex-girlfriends, finally winding around to her footprint tattoos. "Each of the footprints represents an ex-girlfriend. Well," she laughed, "*mostly* ex-girlfriends. One or two boys snuck in there too."

Georgia told me she had tickets to the symphony on Saturday. She wasn't a huge fan of classical music, but her father was, and since he was out-of-town he handed his tickets over. "I like being there when they play classical music. Otherwise, it puts me to sleep. Which I guess isn't always a bad thing," she laughed. "Wanna come along?"

It wasn't until later I found out she was supposed to go with her best friend (and major pogo competitor) Carmen, who loves classical music; she had to trade her two movie nights to change their plans. Carmen had suggested Georgia throw the pogo tournament in trade, but nothing was worth that—not even me, she told me later.

Her father had a platinum membership to the symphony, which included third row seats to every performance. It was the first time I'd seen a symphony this close and been able to watch the faces of the players. The human connection gave the music a certain power I'd never felt before.

It was Beethoven. No idea which symphony. And I'm not

sure I would go to the store and buy it even if I remembered. The feeling I had that night would be impossible to recreate sitting in traffic or baking cookies.

We went out for a Manhattan afterwards—the only cocktail made with sweet vermouth, Georgia told me. "I decided to try a Manhattan a few years back because I figured that if all bars stock a bottle of sweet vermouth for only one drink, it must be a pretty damn good drink. And it is."

"It is good, but I'm a danger on whiskey. Someone once told me that I'm unpredictable on whiskey—which means I'm either very good or very bad."

"Hmm…" Georgia's eyes beamed; she nodded to the bartender for another round. "I'll take my chances."

Before long we were joking about the odd connections people have—like the connection between her name, Georgia, and the art teacher's name, Peach. "Even if Peach hadn't been a kak of mammoth proportion, we never could have dated."

"What's our connection?" I asked, painfully obvious and not yet painfully drunk.

"Well, your full name, Lynn Herr, has as many letters as my last name, Brothers. Plus I think we could wear each other's shoes."

Now, when I'm sober, I think clearly and act reasonably. For example, I know that starting a relationship on a night of drunken sex is bad. I know they rarely last. We were on our third Manhattan, however, so I asked the bartender to call us a cab. Ring up one of those yellow fuckers! *Onward!*

The cab was late, arriving just as we were debating whether to call another one. Five minutes later we pulled up to her house and she tugged me out of the car, telling me there was no way in hell I was going home tonight. Well, alrighty then.

Georgia opened the door with a bit too much gusto and sent her cat's water bowl sailing across the floor, leaving a dangerous line of water in its wake that I naturally slipped in. I grabbed hold of her cookbook shelf and tore it from the wall, then backed into the doorknob and cracked my tail-bone. Thankfully, the Manhattan has been used since ancient times as an anesthetic, so I felt no pain.

She tugged me from the kitchen, through the living room, and directly into bed, where she fumbled with the buttons on her silky ink-stained shirt while I yanked off my shoes, shooting them into the corner with Shaq flare. She left her shirt unbuttoned while she fidgeted with the radio stations, finally sending the entire nation of FM to hell, and popped in a mixed CD with everything from Aztec Camera to Zebra, she told me.

As the music started up, she told me to lie down. "Since (a) I don't know you very well; (b) I'm drunk; and (c) I'm fertile, I'm feeling a little adventuresome. I'm going to make you come without touching you below the waist," she said with a smile.

She spread my arms out and told me that under no cir-cumstances was I to move them. If I did, she would stop. For a few moments I didn't hear the music—I only saw her eyes above mine and felt her cold fingers move slowly over my shirt. I only wore a bra during cold weather and/or PMS; tonight, thankfully, it was neither. She unbuttoned my faux cowboy shirt, laying back each side to reveal my breasts, their pink nipples already alert.

"Have you ever come from nipple play alone?" she asked.

"No…"

"Well, tonight you are going to gain a new appreciation for what these ladies can do." She stood up. "Don't move."

"OK."

Georgia left the room for about five songs. I was begin-ning to think she'd gone and fallen asleep on the couch. Part of me wanted to get up and check, but another part didn't want to risk ruining Nipple Appreciation Night.

Finally she returned, wearing sweatpants and carrying a dark brown wooden tray littered with various treats: a glass of ice, a lit candle, a stick of yellow wax, a small dark jar presumably filled with something fun, and nipple clamps. I'd seen much of this on my travels through sex shops here and there, but hadn't used any. I'd always considered my nipples a fun stop on the way to bigger and better things.

She pulled an eye cover from the back of her sweatpants. "I'm going to put this on. It's best to keep our eyes closed under them so you don't get distracted by flickers of light."

Then, without kissing me, she rubbed my nipples between her finger, pinching them stiff. As her pinches grew harder, I felt a deep stirring in my pussy, back behind my clit. She pulled them both out and twisted hard. I gritted my teeth, enjoying the pain.

Her hands withdrew. Less than a minute later I felt something fall on my right nipple, then a searing heat. At first I thought maybe it was her teeth, but then realized she was dripping hot wax on me. I moved on the bed. "Lay still," she commanded.

Another drop fell on my left nipple. The pain reverberated down the slopes of my breasts; I could imagine progressively lighter red rings of irritation from my nipples outward. They throbbed. And for some reason, my body ached for her fingers. Ached for her to squeeze my nipples again, crack the wax, twist them when they are on fire. Instead she cupped my breasts and kneaded them, sending blood to the tips, increasing the pain of the fire. The pain and the itching and the ache.

My hips pushed up. "No," she told me. "Lie still."

Then she gave me what I wanted; she took each nipple in her fingers and rolled them gently. The wax broke free, pieces of it grinding into my inflamed nipples. I enjoyed the feeling, liked the stabbing. "Harder," I begged.

Without saying a word, the pressure from her fingers increased. I felt every subtle roll over the tops of her thumbs, every soft and hard point. When she twisted and pulled my nipples, stretching them inches above me, my back arched, my pussy tingled. I knew I was wet deep inside. I wanted her to go down on me, but knew I had to keep focus.

She slapped my nipples back down then quickly applied ice to them both. I cried out and the excitement I had just been feeling slid backward. It was cold, so cold over the heat. My jaw hurt from the cold. I felt it through my nipples to my back.

Georgia moved the ice cubes in synchronicity, sending cold streams of water down my breasts. I was shivering, uncomfortable. Then, mercifully, she took the ice away and took my left nipple in her mouth. I moaned. Her tongue warmed my nipple, sending firing jolts of pleasure from my head to the small of my back. She moved to the right nipple. I wanted to reach between my legs.

"Be still."

Cruelly, she replaced the ice cubes on my tender nipples again, then tossed them back in the glass and pressed the cold metal of a clamp down on my left nipple. I was afraid, lying very very still. She slowly tightened the screw on the clamp. I realized that the ice had left my nipples slightly numb, which allowed her to apply a high level of clamp pressure.

After both nipples were clamped, Georgia pulled the chain connecting them, raising me off the bed. "Don't resist," she said. I heard an edge of sadism in her voice, and it excited me.

She tightened the clamps. I felt bee-stings from my nipples directly to my pussy. With both of my nipples stretched in the clamps, Georgia reached behind her and grabbed the ice again. She ran it down my belly, stopping at my pubic line. The pain was intense, but every time I tried to move, she pulled the clamp higher, so within seconds I was trapped perfectly still while she melted most of the remaining ice.

She took the tiny chips, relaxed the chain, and held them on top of my tortured nipples. I felt the wetness inside me seeping out. My clit throbbed.

Georgia released my nipples, which sent small lines of blood to isolated areas, making me intensely aware of the different areas on each nipple—the area in the clamp, above the clamp, below the clamp. Each felt different and alive. She unscrewed the jar behind her, then dabbed a little sticky substance from it on the exposed tops of my nipples.

A few seconds later she began blowing on my nipples, which sent enflamed strands of heat. Each stream of air made the lotion grow hotter until I felt the heat under the clamps, through my skin, and deep inside. Suddenly, I became aware of a growing pressure inside my pussy.

"Close you eyes."

"They are," I told her.

She leaned down and blew again, this time following the air with a flicker of her tongue. I felt that tongue on my clit, and pulled up as I started a slow climax. She raised my nipples up again with the chain, still licking them. I wanted her to touch my pussy, shove her fingers inside me, fuck me. Anything to make this come faster.

"Please—"

I was cut off by a sharp pull that tore pain through my hot breasts and down into my wetness. I was just approaching the edge of an orgasm. I focused on her tongue. I let the rest of my body disappear. The pain and pleasure forced my singular vision.

I was moaning now, frustrated and high. I flew around the edges, unable to get any higher, when Georgia slowly undid the clamps.

As the blood rushed in, my right nipple swelled and throbbed. With each beat, I was pushed higher. The pain pierced my nipple. She stopped and undid the left one to the same degree. Now the pain had no focal point; it flooded my body. I trembled.

Georgia released my right nipple from the clamp. It sprung back, swelling and burning. Then my left. An orgasm was on upon me now—flowing through my body, a long plateau. Then she took both nipples in her fingers and squeezed. I screamed out as I reached a high I'd never felt before. I came and came. She maintained her position, holding with the exact same pressure until I stopped moaning.

After I'd settled into the bed, she slowly slowly let go of my nipples. They were tired, sensitive, irritated, and happy. She removed my eye covering, and kissed me tenderly on the mouth.

"Don't thank me. Thank the ladies," she said with a grin.

"This is the first time I think I really met the ladies."

"Then we should name them."

"How about… Rosie—after the color—and Georgia."

"Well, I'm flattered," Georgia said.

"Rosie and Georgia," I repeated.

"Yes," she laughed. "We've already met."

making the best | beth greenwood

I couldn't sleep. I was exhausted, weary, wrung out—all of that—but not sleepy. I knew I should be, more than anything because I still had to get up in the morning, but I simply wasn't. Closing my eyes didn't help because after a few moments they'd be open and I'd be staring up at the unfamiliar ceiling again.

If I'd been back in my little place off Melrose, the terracotta bungalow with the dirt-filled flower boxes. I could have watched television, done tai chi, even had a drink. But I wasn't in that hot, noisy little 1940s box; I wasn't home.

The dust made me sneeze, the bent blinds would never come clean no matter how much I scrubbed, and the toilet would run and run and run for hours at a time. But it had been home, my home, and I missed it. The missing was an ache, a fist in my chest.

I'm not going to cry, I thought, looking up at the ceiling with the cheap gold fixture in the middle. *Done enough of that.*

Home. I managed a sly smile despite the heavy sadness. *You can't go home again*, I thought—but that's exactly where I was; I just wasn't in the home I wanted.

A board creaked and I bit my lip. Had I made too much noise? Mom had never been a heavy sleeper and seemed to get even more fragile as she got older. "Mama's going to try and sleep—be careful now," Dad always said. To Mom, even breaking eggshells sounded like pistol shots, so I didn't dare walk even on them. One of the first things I'd done once I'd gotten my money together and finally—*finally*—moved out was to buy the biggest, loudest stereo I could.

The board creaked again. No, not Mom—just the house settling. I let out the breath I'd been unconsciously holding, ballooned cheeks shrinking as I slowly blew up at the ceiling. I spotted a few cobwebs waving in the breeze and the wry smile returned.

After a few minutes I relaxed again, drifting back into my insomnia. I catalogued what I still had to do: move boxes, sell more stuff, go through my clothes and pick out what to keep, what to give to Goodwill. The stereo. I hoped I could get some good money for it.

I closed my eyes, not tired. I kept them shut until, after a few more slow breaths, I knew I wouldn't cry.

My eyes dried a bit and I sniffled—only once—then went back to staring up at the ceiling: ugly brass fixture, cobweb, peeling paint in the far right corner. After a while I wasn't sad—well, not as sad—just bored.

Then I was really bored. Then I started to get horny.

Without anything else to occupy my thoughts, I started drifting into how my body was feeling lying on the futon, on the floor, the scratchy blanket, T-shirt, panties. The way my feet stuck out at the bottom—I was usually the tallest girl wherever I went—the cool hardwood on the tips of my toes. The way my nails scratched against the floor, catching in the whorls of the grain as I stretched, trying to get comfortable.

As I turned, rolling back and forth, my tits pressed into the futon, rubbing against the soft cotton of my shirt, and my undies gripped and tugged between the cheeks of my ass.

Fuck, I thought, when I realized I was actually wet. A quick finger confirmed it. *Oh, fuck.*

I knew myself pretty well. Loud music made me happy, strong coffee was the only thing that could wake me up in the morning, lemon soap made me feel really clean, salsa gave me a stomachache—and once I was wet, really wet. There was just no going back.

Besides, I thought to myself, *maybe I'll finally be able to get to fucking sleep.*

When I was a kid, first exploring the warm, soft, wet folds between my legs (and then that special little bead down there), I didn't have anything but fantasies to push me up and over the top. But in the little terra-cotta bungalow, the first home I'd had all to myself, that'd changed. Now it had to be something real, something I'd actually touched, tasted, felt, to get me off.

In the first months it had been near encounters, a kiss here and there, a bout of sofa humping, maybe a flash of tit at some raucous club. But I couldn't think about that kind of thing anymore. No, the only thing that worked really well—and quickly—was thinking of Nancy.

Deftly, old training coming easily, I reached under the comforter and hooked my thumbs into my panties. Knees up, pushing the panties forward, over, and then off, I paused, a sudden heat flash of giddy nastiness: back home, panties off, pussy very wet.

Then I frowned, almost slamming a fist down onto the futon; damn mother's so-fragile sleep! My eyes started to itch from hot tears, and I really wanted to cry. But I didn't. Instead I whistled in a few more slow breaths, calming myself down. Sleep was what I needed, wanted. Sleep first—everything else could wait till morning. Sleep, but first, a good come—and that meant Nancy.

A little pressure and my lips parted, welcoming the intimate gesture, rewarding me with the hot slick wetness. *Damned horny*, I thought.

Nancy. Strong coffee, lemon soap, salsa, loud music—and Nancy. The first time I'd had seen her it was like I'd been waiting all my life for her but hadn't been aware of it. If anyone had asked me, and no one had, I would've said I'd fall for someone femme and colorful, full of catchy pop tunes and heartfelt lesbian values.

Instead, there was Nancy. Not really butch—not classically, anyway—but definitely not something Disney would model a doll after. I stretched a finger up, grazing my clit—and a shiver raced back and forth from my crotch to the top of my head.

That first night...what was it, six months ago? I'd been making my way through L.A., one dyke club after another, when I came across the Cat House. Open mic night at the Cat House, specifically. Poetry about cats and doing bad things to certain politicians, lots of stuff about bleeding and womenhood, or womynhood, or whatever the spelling of the month was. I don't know why I stayed. I wasn't looking for poetry but rather something pounding, drumming, loud, brassy, and powerful.

My hand was on the door, the coughs and scattered polite applause from the last performer still behind me. For some reason I didn't walk out, for some reason I turned around to see who was up next.

Wet, very wet—I slipped a finger in, moving it slowly around where lips became the throat of my cunt. It was good feeling, something private and very hot. I wanted to moan, to hiss, but instead just bit my lip—I could have made all the noise I wanted if I was back home, but here, in Mom's house, mum was the word.

Nancy was up next. Tall—maybe even taller than me—with hair the color of soot-covered straw, a pair of quarter-size blue glasses hiding her eyes, tight black jeans, a torn-up T-shirt with barely legible PUSSY PATROL printed on it. As she walked up to the microphone, I saw apple-size breasts sway beneath. Instantly, without knowing her name or even caring what it was, I wanted to reach up under that shirt and give them a squeeze.

Then she spoke. The club had been a cavern, a crypt—like

I said, dull—but then she started. I can't remember what she said, what poetry she read or story she told. None of the words stuck in my brain—but two things did: She was fucking hot, and she was gloriously loud.

After, as she stepped off to a momentary stunned silence and then a sudden crash of shocked applause, she headed over to the bar. "Water," she said, her voice raspy, strained by her performance. Even roughed up, her voice was muscled, tight, sexy. Watching her drink I instantly wanted to hear her say certain special things to me with it. Things that would accompany certain special shared activities.

One finger around the tight bead of my clit. Now, every time I touch it, I think of Nancy.

Nancy, the tall girl who turned to me and said, "One for you too? Sometimes I think listening to me read must be as exhausting as me reading."

We sat and drank, not really having much to say at first. Looking back, I know we didn't have to say anything. She was aware, but I wasn't, that we were trying each other out, seeing if there was something there.

There was. After downing her Calistoga, she took my hand and said, voice still sounding like she'd gargled with sand, "Let's go somewhere."

I loved my clit. Big, hard, and wonderfully sensitive—too sensitive to touch dry, so I swirled a finger in my hot juices and rubbed slowly, carefully around it. The feeling was incredible, and I had to bite my lip again to keep from easing out a nice, good moan.

We went somewhere. Since she'd been sofa-surfing at some friends', it was my terra-cotta bungalow. My dusty, dirty home—my first guest. My first guest, my first—and best—lover.

At the door, after she gave the place a quick look over and I shrank, shrank, shrank seeing the dishes in the sink, the futon still folded down, butterfly-stained panties wadded on the floor, trash baskets overflowing. "Nice place," she'd said, without sarcasm. I'd smiled at that, knowing that here was a kindred spirit: dirty, noisy, cheap. It was a good home. My home.

Time for a good, quick rub. Time to circle my clit and enjoy the wonderful feelings surging up and down my body. I arched my back, relishing it all. Of course God's a woman: Who else would have invented such a wonderful thing as a clit?

Nancy kissed me. In my little home. One minute we were smiling and laughing, sitting on my hastily folded futon, and the next she was close—so close I felt her hot breath on my cheek—and then we were kissing. I'd kissed before, but this wasn't playful kissing. This kiss was an invitation, a door that was really going to open. I got wet, really wet, soaking my panties in a flood.

More rubbing. God, yes, good rubbing around and around the sweet little knot, making me curl my toes, tense my arms and legs. My tits ached for a touch, any touch. One hand now, my right, up under my shirt. My tits aren't big, but I like them—especially when I'm rubbing myself. A stroke, at first, under the soft skin, thinking of Nancy, and then flickering fingers over the tight rubber of my nipple. Good, so damned good.

Then she said those sweet words, the words that for the longest time would push me right over the edge, heave me into a moaning, bellowing come: "You're really wet right now, aren't you?"

I hadn't said anything. I hadn't even nodded.

Time for a nipple. Gently at first, then with a good pinch. The wonderful ache zapped down through my tit, joining the rolling thunder coming up from my cunt. I wheezed, no longer caring if I woke the dead—or more importantly my mom. A come, a really good come, was close—so close I could taste it. "Taste," and that word made me think again of Nancy.

"Let's see if that's true, eh?" she'd said, kissing me again for what felt like a decade or two. Away from my mouth, her hand dropped down to the crotch of my jeans, starting a pulsing squeeze. I remember moaning, catching the sound deep in my throat as I always had, allowing out only the tiniest of mews.

She pulled off my shoes, tossing them aside like shucked oysters, laughing. I giggled along but couldn't move. I was too shocked and too excited to risk doing anything that could make her stop the wonderful things she'd been doing.

My legs and arms ached as I pinched and rubbed. As I pinched and rubbed, my back arched and my heels grazed the hard floor. As my heels grazed the floor I thought about Nancy.

My jeans had come off at last. My panties were old and holey; I remembered blushing, suddenly even hotter. But they didn't stay on long, for Nancy—quick and sure and smiling all the time—reached under my ass and took hold of the elastic.

I'd flexed, tightened my ass cheeks—and in the guest room of my mom's house I did the same. I'd lifted my ass, letting this strange girl take my panties off—and in the guest room of my mom's house I lifted my ass—wishing Nancy were there with me.

I'd thought about what it would be like, of course. I had my myths: romance, true love, perfect tits (hers or mine). I'd never imagined someone like Nancy, and that made it so much better. New home, new places, new things—I'd grown up. Time to start living.

But first...silence. Quiet in my mom's house (again) and quiet back then in my home. Reverent silences both places, both times. Back then, though, it'd been broken by Nancy: "Such a nice pussy. Such a lovely cunt."

A night for first kisses. My first one that led to sex, then the first kiss that *was* sex. I thought I'd explode, that first time—the first time her lips dropped down and innocently, then not so innocently, kissed me between my thighs. But I didn't explode. Nothing premature for my first time. No. One lick, two licks, three flicks, four...

Mirrors in time: back then and right then in my mom's room. One lick, one good stroke, two licks, two good strokes, three good licks, three fantastic strokes. Then and now, the come had loomed, something powerful, wonderful, and oh-so-hot.

Back then, with Nancy, I'd screamed—bellowed out my joy, my pleasure, set off my own special fireworks with my voice. Speaking aloud, yelling that it was good. And it was good to be alive, for the first time.

But when my come came there in my mom's guest room I was silent and stifled—I kept it in, bit it back, stuffed it down deep. I moaned, just a little, but that was all. Afterward, quietly panting, the world was too quiet. The world back to normal—the normal I'd learned to hate.

Sleep now. The memory of my best time, my hottest time, flicking around my crackling, popping mind.

Then the tears did come, silent as everything else. Swallowed sobs when I remembered the rest of it. Nancy's smile. Kissing Nancy, making love to Nancy. Looking into Nancy's eyes.

One day Nancy was gone.

Sleep now. Sadness and sleep. More moving in the morning, having to leave my real home behind, having to move back in with Mom.

Sleep. Someday soon I hoped I'd be out again, alive again.

But for now, sleep.

your hands | sharon wachsler

I don't know if this is a typical "woman thang" or if it's just my peculiarity, but I always wake up wet. It's not about my dreams; I could be dreaming about a trigonometry test or falling from a bridge. Maybe it was partly being with you, having you in my bed every night, that set my internal clock to "turned on" every morning. It's still true now. Maybe this is a way you have changed me forever, even though it's been 10 years since I've seen you. Even though you've changed your name now, transitioned, I've heard, into a boi.

To me, you will always be the way I remember you that morning, like so many other mornings. Once my eyes open, I am awake. You, however, could sleep through all your morning classes and some of the afternoon's too. This morning, I decided to do something. You awakened so much in me—passion, living in the moment, the joy of risks. On this morning, in my way, I wanted to waken you.

❧

It's still dark. To my bleary unaided eye it looks like the clock says 6:30. I don't want to put my glasses on and spoil the mood. If I see you too clearly, I won't do what I want; I won't completely give in to my fetish.

You're asleep on your back, your arms and legs splayed,

taking up as much of the queen-size futon as one human being can. Your arm is tossed above my head. I slide in toward you, pulling that arm across my chest and examining your hand.

I smile at how large your hands are, even in comparison to the rest of you—not gangly hands with long fingers, but smooth cocoa skin and firm palms and flat, short fingernails. I know my hand fetish embarrasses you a little, so I rarely comment on how fine I find your fingers.

Besides, talk is cheap. I sink in. Your pinkie is so sweet, I can't help myself. I start there. I kiss the tip very lightly, then run it gently around my lips, up my cheek and across my forehead, down my other cheek, and across my lips. I really want to taste you, but I wait. I pull your fingers to my mouth and bring the little one in. I start sucking carefully on the end, feeling the tiny ridges in the nail with my bottom lip. Then down further, bringing it up and down against my lips. You stir a little. I look over but you are still asleep.

I take your finger in again, this time moving it all the way in so that I feel the nail at my throat. I bring it in and out, sucking harder, running my teeth along the underside.

My eyes are closed, but I hear you moan. I wriggle, making sure you feel my breasts against your arm. On each of your fingers I perform my ritual, moving from your bare "ring finger" to my favorite, your index finger. I don't know if a finger can be called muscular, but if it can, this is it. I'm a sucker for a well-muscled woman.

At some point your body has followed your hand and you're pressed up against my side. It feels nice, but I'm not ready to acknowledge the rest of you yet. I lick your thumb, around and around in circles from the top down to the base, then suddenly suck it to the back of my throat. You gasp.

I kiss you in circles on your palm, starting at the base of each finger and moving down into the center. Then my tongue follows, licking in circles, until I sink into the meaty pad beneath your thumb, sucking and biting. You press into me closer, trying to move your hand from my mouth to my breast. I make *tsk tsk* sounds, bringing your errant hand to my mouth again, sucking on your index finger, slowly and strongly.

"Oh, God," you exhale, falling back, then scramble to climb on top of me. I say nothing, but push you back onto the bed.

With sharp teeth I nibble across your palm and down to your wrist, sucking there above the blue veins. I love the sensation of the blood flowing just beneath. I wish I could taste it, feel it pulsing through me. You stifle a groan. With quick bites down the underside of your arm, I inch closer to you until I am at your armpit. I run my tongue around the kinked, silky hair.

You reach for me again, with your free hand, trying to slip it between my legs. I intercept and bring it above your head, looking down at your open eyes for the first time. You smile and raise an eyebrow. Sleepy, turned-on butch. I bring your other hand above your head also, and lean there with my weight on my elbows, pinning your hands. We both know you could flip me if you wanted to.

Deliberately, I look down at your chest, at your breasts beneath the white ribbed tank top. I stare so hard that I can see your nipples move. You're waiting for my habitual next step: to climb on top of you and suck you through the cloth. But this morning it's my game.

I continue to lean over you on one arm. With the other I lift your tank top over your head and wrap it around your wrists. My breasts dangle in your face and you try to grab one in your mouth. I think better of it and stay to your side. Keeping one hand on the tank-top restraint, I nuzzle up to your ear.

"Darling," I whisper, very low.

"I woke up very horny and wet this morning. I'd love for you to feel how wet, but..."

You strain to catch my words, but I tilt down to suck on your earlobe and bite your neck, your weak spot. I feel you tense, holding back.

I'm back at your ear. "But not yet. I do want you to fuck me. I really want you to fuck me. I can't wait to feel you inside me…"

You moan, "Come on, baby," forgetting the tank top around your wrists, and roll onto me. I roll you back.

"I'm not finished," I say in my best haughty bitch voice.

You make a noise—somewhere between a groan and a chuckle. I ignore it and run my tongue down the side of your torso. You stop chuckling. I make circles around your navel, spreading my mouth over your stomach, pretending not to see your breasts. I move up your sternum. Sucking at the V at the base of your throat I grab the waistband of your boxers. You lift your hips and I yank them off.

With my mouth at your throat, I brush your nipple with my hand—as if by accident—on my way to your thigh. You push your breast up to meet me, but I'm no longer there. My index finger traces down from your hip bone to the opening of your vagina, over and over again. As you tremble, I drop my full mouth over your breast and pull in, filling my whole mouth. You cry out and, tossing off the tank top, hook your arms across my back and your legs around my thighs, rocking.

Bending toward my face you breathe, "I want you. I want you." I bite your nipple hard, feeling it give, then stiffen beneath my front teeth, then suck again. You shudder and utter a low yelp.

I decide to give in this time. "I want you too."

You pounce. Frenziedly, you tear off my underwear and T-shirt. I am aching, fully ready. I can see the sun starting to glow off the snow outside the window.

But now you've got me where you want me.

"What do you want?" you ask, as if you needed clarification.

We're naked, my face in your neck, and I feel one of your hands around my ass, the other on the inside of my thigh. So close.

"Oh, please." I rock from side to side, embarrassed, turned on.

"Yes, but what do you want?" You're making circles on my thigh and on my ass with your fingers. I want them in my mouth again. We lock eyes. For the second time this morning you smile in that way, raising one eyebrow.

The drumming and circling of your fingers makes me dizzy. I'm squirming, grinding against you. I don't know when that started. "Please, oh, please." I can't concentrate. "I want you inside me."

You remove your hand from my thigh, and I gasp, expecting it against my clit. Instead you're stroking my cheek. I turn and draw you in hungrily, lost in the rhythm of rocking and sliding your finger in and out of my mouth.

"What do you want? What do you want?" Your voice is husky, mesmerizing.

I moan over and over, your finger against my tongue.

"Fuck me. Please, oh, please. Fuck me..." Before I can get the last word out I am yelling, your fingers finally in my cunt, your thumb on my clit.

I've been waiting for this moment for years. I can only yell and yell, hoping to draw you in further, to engulf you from both ends. One hand in my mouth, the other in my cunt, I'm filled with you, with your hands, your hands pounding in and out, the slippery friction, the heat, my swollen clit. I lose track of time and sensation.

I feel a trickle running into my ass, and the sharp edge of a fingernail somewhere, and I'm coming and coming and coming. Somebody is yelling, and as my orgasm subsides I realize it's me.

I know I'll hear about this from my housemates. My room is right next to the kitchen, with a two-inch gap under the door. The sound flows right out; we might as well have been fucking on the kitchen table for all the privacy we get.

Still, we hold each other. I kiss your shoulder and your chin. You run a finger down my nose. I put on my glasses. The clock says 8:30. I need to be out the door to my sociology class in 45 minutes. I spring out of bed.

"See you tonight," you mumble, and roll over to sleep.

I meander into the kitchen, which is mercifully empty. W. and E. must still be asleep. Or trying to fall back asleep. Maybe they just don't want to face me after my operatic performance.

&

I shuffle toward campus, thinking of your hands, how I want them tied with something stronger than a tank top. How next time when I flip you, you will stay flipped. I want them available for my pleasure, for hours, the rest of you bound. I decide to place an order with that store in San Francisco. It's time to invest in some very large, very strong restraints. I can taste your fingers already.

redirect | heather towne

"I think you'll find most everything there, Brenda."

"Thank you, Roy. If Heather and I need anything else, we'll let you know." She handed him a cool smile.

He wasn't easily discouraged. He leered back. "OK, good." He hesitated at the boardroom door. "I'm just down the hall—third door on the right." He pointed. "My door's always open for you two ladies."

Brenda picked up a file and glanced through it. "We know where your office is. Thanks again."

Roy slowly took the hint. He adjusted his wire-rim glasses, patted his comb-over, then slid out the door.

"Oh, Roy!"

He quickly filled the door again. "Yes, Brenda?"

"Could you close the door, please?"

He frowned and shut the door.

I couldn't help laughing. "I think he likes you," I said.

Brenda looked at me and smiled. "Roy tries to 'like' all the women from our firm. Why don't you pull up a chair and we can start going through these files? We don't want to keep Roy here all night. He has a family waiting at home, after all."

I pushed my stuff over on the table, closer to Brenda. The gleaming surface of the oak table was littered with files, ledgers, receipts, and invoices. Brenda picked up a thick file labeled SHANAHAN TRUCKING and handed it to me. "Remember," she said, "we're looking for anything that would indicate there was more than the usual business relationship between our client and the Shanahan group of companies—especially as it relates to the purchase of Ackland Chemical." She looked at me. "Got it?"

"Got it," I replied.

Brenda is a senior partner at the firm. I was delighted and shocked to be working with her—most of the partners didn't even know the names of their articling students. But Brenda had initially recruited me and had taken a special interest in me ever since.

We pored over the documentation; Brenda jotted down notes on a legal pad. I flipped through files, giving her everything that might be important, made photocopies, and carried ledgers back and forth from Roy's office and the accounting department.

"How much longer do you think you'll be?" Roy asked, as I handed him a binder.

"I'd say about another hour."

Roy glanced at the big, macho watch on his bony left wrist. "Eight o'clock, eh. OK, I'll phone 'she who cooks the dinner' and let her know."

His fingers touched mine when I handed him an accordion file full of receipts. He grinned.

"See you later," I said.

He frowned.

I went back to the boardroom and plopped down in the chair next to Brenda. "I think Roy is after *me* now."

Brenda glanced up and laughed. "Well, you are a very pretty girl," she said as she patted my shoulder. Her hand was warm. "Wow. I'm starting to get tired. How about you?"

"Um, no, I'm not too tired." I smiled shyly and looked down at some papers. Brenda thought I was pretty! I'd had a crush on her since day one. Since then we'd gone for drinks with the group a few times after work, but I'd always seen a distance in her eyes—until lately, that is. I'd noticed how she looked at me around the office—like maybe she had more than just my professional growth in mind. Or maybe I was just fooling myself. There was only one way to find out. I sucked up some courage and quietly asked. "You really think I'm pretty?"

"Sorry?"

"Uh, you said I was a very pretty girl...and..." I blushed crimson.

She stared at me, her clear, sky-blue eyes penetrating mine. Then she smiled and said, "You're more than pretty. You're beautiful." She leaned closer, reached over, and gently lifted my chin.

My body grew warm and heavy all of a sudden, and my lips parted on their own as her soft fingers began to caress my face.

"You need to have confidence in your abilities," she whispered, her breath hot on my face, her lips only inches from mine. "I do."

I was about to mumble something inane when she kissed me lightly on the lips. I gulped, and my body trembled. I couldn't believe she had just kissed me!

"I'm sorry," she said as she pulled away.

"No, please. I want you to—"

Then she kissed me again. I felt dizzy and the room grew hot. Her perfume was smothering me, inviting and intoxicating. She got up, rolled a chair over to the boardroom door, and jammed it under the doorknob. She slowly walked back to me, her eyes on mine. I watched breathlessly as she took off her jacket and draped it over the back of her chair. She grasped my right hand and brought me to my feet. My legs felt weak. I didn't know what was going to happen next; things were happening so fast. She stood close to me and kissed me again, longer this time. Her soft lips pressed against mine and I moaned.

"Are you sure this is all right?" she asked.

"Positive."

I felt one of her hands gently cup my left breast, squeezing it slightly. I gasped and awkwardly flung my arms around her, pulling her body hard against mine. I opened my mouth and felt her tongue. I tingled all over. I felt her large breasts press against mine, our nipples touching through the thin fabric of our clothing.

Brenda is about 40 years old and has a slim, toned body. Her breasts, however, are large and heavy. She has black hair cut fairly short, and a delicate, sensitive face. We stood there, in the middle of the boardroom, locked in a passionate embrace, fiercely kissing each other. I thanked God the windows were frosted glass.

Brenda's hands explored my breasts, then she suddenly stepped back. I opened my eyes and saw she was unbuttoning my top. I was wearing a simple white blouse and a simple black skirt. She slowly unfastened all the buttons, pulled the hem of the blouse out of my skirt, then pushed the garment open. The cool air felt good against my overheated body. She ran her hands through my long, blond hair as she stood there admiring me, her eyes sparkling.

Her fingers drifted over my face, my lips, my neck, my shoulders, my breasts. I felt Brenda unhook my bra. "Very nice," she murmured.

She pushed the bra and the blouse over my shoulders and they slid down my back and dropped onto the carpet. I squeezed my breasts together and rolled the long, hard nipples between my fingers. "Please," I moaned. "Suck my tits."

Brenda bent forward, gently removed my hands, and teased my nipples with her tongue, flicking her tongue lightly against each nipple, making them stiffer still. My body quivered. She began sucking on my breasts, first one, then the other. She bathed my breasts with her hot tongue and bit lightly on my rock-hard nipples. She sucked hard on my breast, tugging on the nipple with her teeth. I looked down at Brenda working my engorged nipples with her mouth and tongue and shuddered in amazement.

Brenda was my boss, for goodness sake, and a partner in one of the largest and most prestigious law firms in the city. But not now—now she was my lover, and my pussy was soaking wet.

"Ready for more?" she asked.

Before I could answer, she pushed me back onto the table, clearing the papers away, until all I felt was the cool tabletop against my back. She leaned over top of me and we kissed ferociously. I stretched my arms back over my head, arching my back, surrendering my body to Brenda. She could do what she wanted.

She slowly kissed and licked her way down my naked body, stopping to suck again on my swollen nipples. I bit my lip and moaned. I felt her wet tongue in my navel and gasped. She put my legs together and pulled off my panties. Her hands roamed over and between my legs. Her pink tongue flicked across my skin, raising goose bumps wherever it went.

"Yes," I whispered, struggling to keep from exploding.

Brenda responded by spreading my legs. She rested my legs on her shoulders and blew softly on my wet pussy. It only fanned my raging fire. When her moist tongue touched me, I moaned loudly. I didn't care if there were a hundred people in the building and they were all watching me. All I knew was that Brenda's tongue was pushing into me.

"God, you taste great," Brenda murmured.

Her voice vibrated throughout my whole body. Her tongue flickered faster over me.

"I'm coming!" I screamed.

She grabbed my ass and lifted me off the table, her tongue plowing harder over my clit and I cried, "Yes!"

My body went rigid as the sexual tension reached a boiling point.

I madly rolled my nipples between my fingers. My body spasmed uncontrollably. Two orgasms tore through my body.

After a few quiet moments I opened my eyes. I had never come so intensely in my entire life. I smiled weakly at Brenda. She stood up and unbuttoned her top and unhooked her bra.

"Care to redirect, counselor?" she asked playfully, a wicked smile dancing across her lips.

"But of course," I said, wondering if I should tell Roy he might miss dinner altogether.

...and liberty for all |
stephanie schroeder

She flashed that devilish smile when she met me at a coffee shop after work. "Let's get the hell outta here!"

I grabbed my bags, including the small shopping bag with
the toys I had bought just for this evening. I shrugged on my
coat and met her outside the door. "Hi. It's nice to see you
again," I smiled, a little hesitant. I hopped into her car as she
pumped the sound and the heat.

"It's nice to see you again too," she finally replied, breaking the awkward silence.

❧

This wintry New York night had been planned via e-mail
after we'd met online a few days earlier. Just a simple: "Hi,
how are you? I'd like to make some new friends in New
York," in my inbox. I wrote her from my office. A short note
at first, but then it grew and grew until it became an elucida-
tion on butch-femme dynamics.

That had been the hook for me: She had checked "butch"
in the "identifies as" slot on her accompanying personals pro-
file and had left out her weight—which to me meant "big
butch." Perfect.

❧

Sitting in her car driving to the hourly motel that she suggested, I felt free. And crazy. Jesus, I had a partner at home, a long-term relationship of ten years. And a four-year-old son. And here I was, in a car with a woman I barely knew, on a sexual adventure, a feverish escapade—and charade: She believed me to be a high femme, and for that night I was. Me, with a real butch, a woman who often passed for a guy, wore men's clothing, and had a penchant for conventionally pretty, slim brunettes. I was on a fantasy journey of getting laid by a butch in an hourly motel in Manhattan's meat-packing district.

❧

Earlier that week, we discussed the mechanics of the scene via e-mail—what we liked and didn't like, and latex. Very important, latex. I scored some blue gloves from the café downstairs and bought condoms at the bodega on the corner. I also bought a dick for the occasion, she having said that her inventory was low and the only available dildo was "a brown one that I use for anybody."

"Well, I'm not anybody," I told her, typing rapidly on my keyboard. "I'll bring my own." I chose "Bogart," a six-inch purple silicone cock purchased from the local sex-toy store.

And then I got cold feet. Maybe she was a serial killer, or maybe she would turn away from me because of my Tourette's, or, or, or.... So, I invited her to lunch. "Near your office," I offered. "I'll take a cab down on my lunch hour."

❧

For at least two years I'd been discussing with my therapist my increasingly insistent desire to have an affair. But the question was always with whom, and how. My partner kept a tight leash on me, so I set up an online personals account at work. I put up my glam model head shot over the weekend, and by Monday morning I had a dozen inquiries. Most of them were interesting women, some of whom I'm a still friends with, but never a butch. Until this one.

When I e-mailed her, I wrote and wrote and wrote. I asked her what I thought I needed to know from a butch, especially one I was going to fuck, or rather, who was going to fuck me: "Do you own your cock?" I asked. "Because, I mean, it's one thing for just any lesbian to strap on a dildo, but quite another for a butch to own her cock." I had told her my friend Joan had told me this and my friend Joan was very experienced in this area.

❧

When I met her at lunch, I brought her an autographed copy of *A Fragile Union* along with my modeling composite card as a bookmark and reminder. "*This* is your friend Joan?" she asked. "Joan Nestle? The one you referred to in your e-mail? The expert on butch and femme?"

"Um-hum," I said. "She's taught me quite a bit. A lot about sexual dynamics between women, about finding—and acting on—my real desires, my deep-down cravings and how to have a rip-roaring time while on my back with my knees over my ears."

She smiled broadly. Our orders came, and I devoured my food. When I had gobbled up my meal, I looked her square in the eye for the first time since we had met and said, "Betcha didn't think I was going to finish it, didya?"

"Well, no," she said.

"I'm not one of those skinny model chicks who never eats or only chews celery sticks or throws everything up after my meal. I've got great metabolism. I probably eat more than you do."

She smiled and said she imagined I did. She told me how beautiful I was and asked if I was I still comfortable meeting later that night. "Of course I am," I asserted. "I'm very excited."

"Good," she said, and paid the bill like a gallant butch.

We walked out, back to her office. I saw her slyly pop a mint into her mouth. Yes! That meant a kiss. And yes, she did kiss me—with tongue, if you must know, and I had to push her away. Not because I wanted her to stop. I didn't, not at all. In that quick moment all of my long, pent-up desire came rushing forth and I didn't want to stop. But I was running late.

I jumped into a cab and made it back to my office without anyone noticing my absence.

❧

Later that evening we pulled into a parking spot on the edge of a warehouse. PRIME-CUT BEEF, the sign on the building read. *Appropriate,* I thought to myself.

She took my hand, and we walked arm-in-arm around the corner. The Liberty Inn was discreetly lit and situated on a little knoll in the middle of four bisecting streets. A tiny pirate's paradise island in the middle of the buzzing city where I was going to get some booty.

My heart leapt as she opened the door for me: I was gonna get laid by a butch! And that meant I was having an affair. Or, this being a one-night stand, I would be cheating.

My date paid by credit card and signed her own name. "I'm single," she explained. "I don't have to worry." The clerk couldn't have been more bored; he barely looked up from his Stephen King novel. "Here, Room 3, through that door and to the left." I tightly gripped my tiny shopping bag of pleasure tools.

She turned the key to the room. It was very clean and minimalist with a burgundy bed and a desk and chair. There was a small bathroom with a shower stall off to the right with a matching burgundy curtain. All in all, decent digs at $53 for two hours. My curfew was midnight, and it was now about 9 o'clock.

❧

My big handsome butch stared at me from the bed. "You are gorgeous," she said in a carnal whisper.

I straddled her legs and kissed her. Deep kisses, tongue kisses, slurpy, messy, yummy kisses. She slid her hands under my silk sweater and pinched my nipples. It felt so good to be touched again somewhat roughly. My butch peeled off my skintight blue sweater then slowly unzipped my pants. She pulled them all way the down as I bent over to remove the bunch around my ankles. She gave me a slap on the bottom. It was her signal. "Give me the dildo," she commanded. I handed her the small shopping bag with the goods wrapped in delicate green Christmas tissue paper. "I'll be right back," she said, and disappeared into the bathroom, returning a minute later with her boxers full of cock and a white jogging bra binding her breasts.

It was the first time I had really seen her body. She was quite big but very firm. A butch goddess bearing the tools for my pleasure. "Lie down," she said. I immediately lay back on the edge of the bed. She pulled on a blue glove. It tore—too small. I had also brought a few surgical gloves. She put on one of those: a perfect fit. She brushed my bush, and I got even wetter. She smiled devilishly; she was having fun.

She fingered me open and pushed in, slowly and softly at first and then a hard thrust. Then more fingers. She roughly finger-fucked me until I came. "Now it's show-time," she announced, and, like a peacock strutting its stuff, pulled out her cock—well, mine, really—and slathered it with lube that was sitting on the adjacent nightstand. She rubbed the remainder on my cunt. I inhaled deeply as she positioned herself between my legs and took hold of her member, expertly guiding it directly between my now-puffy sensitive pussy lips.

She pushed, and I pushed, and the cock slid in slowly, and when I had engulfed her she started thrusting like a pro. She pumped and I bucked, fucking back. I was full of her, gushing like the lower estuary of the Hudson River. My eyes were closed and I was in the moment—enveloping her thickness and enjoying her refined technique. Every push sent wet, hard echoes through my belly.

She said something barely audible. Apparently she thought I wasn't into it because I seemed disconnected, in my own world. "No," I gasped, "this is the best fuck I've ever had. It sent me into my own head space."

She nodded, then continued to hammer, pump, and thrust until I came and came and came. Then she pulled out and, oh, that pleasure-pain of withdrawal: It was exquisite! My butch threw herself across the bed, exhausted, spent. I lay next to her for a while, quiet, our breathing in sync. Then she grabbed my face and pulled me toward her. "Goddamn it, that was great," she told me. For the first time I noticed the gold flecks in her brown eyes. "You are so light and flexible. It was incredible how I could just lift you onto my dick right at the edge of the bed."

I wanted to cry tears of joy, of freedom, but instead I put my mouth to hers and we shared a long, deeply passionate kiss.

❧

The Liberty Inn. Bogart. A butch's checkered boxers with an expensive custom-made leather harness underneath. The tenderness in the kiss of this virtual stranger. My fantasy had been fulfilled.

What had just passed between us would be burned into my memory forever. This big butch first buying me lunch at noon, then arriving that evening wearing a man's suit to pick me up from my vanilla androgynous world and transport me into hers. Ours. An intimate connection in the middle of the chaos and constant, sometimes annoying, buzz that is New York City.

she loves me | elaine miller

I'm not much of a copycat, but I know a brilliant idea when I hear one.

The top in a couple I knew wanted to express to the bottom exactly what a well-behaved submissive she was, and so declared a single day where no *good* deeds would go unpunished. I know it sounds back-asswards, but at the end of the long, painful day, with her buttocks glowing red like the light bulb over a whore's bed, my submissive friend knew she was a very good grrl indeed. And if she had a moment of doubt over the next few days, why, she'd only have to sit down to be reminded all over again.

My own beautiful and talented butch bottom, Spike, has the occasional crisis of faith, where it's hard for her to understand how well-loved she is. Inspired by my friends' success story, I believed I had just the way to reassure her for a long time to come. I made careful preparations and told Spike to expect a very difficult scene on Saturday night.

On Saturday I spent hours before her punctual arrival making myself as beautiful as I could, setting up the playroom to be just right, and dragging all my equipment out. I also wrote two notes.

One was for the outside of the door. It read: "Spike: Let yourself in, close the door behind you, lock and chain it."

The second one, placed just inside the door, read: "Turn off the lights upstairs. Come right downstairs to the playroom. Don't knock—just come in."

After taping the notes in place, I slipped on a floor-length clinging black dress and five-inch heels. I reasoned that if I were going to cause my lover the amount of physical distress I was planning, she ought to have something lovely to look at while she was suffering. Not exactly a consolation prize, but you catch my drift.

I slipped downstairs and lit the candles, then spent some time adjusting the chains hanging from the ceiling. I'm always nervous before a big date. Don't ever let anyone tell you tops are always as cool as cucumbers; we dither like anyone else.

When I heard her key turn in the lock upstairs, my heart stopped for a moment. I arranged myself hurriedly to look composed—no, languid—in a chair against the far wall of the playroom. The sound of her boots marked the firm, measured step of the truly terrified; I fancied I could hear her heart beating.

With barely a pause, she stepped into the room. She'd outdone herself in the cute butch grooming department. Her black boots gleamed softly in the reddish light of my playroom, her perfectly scruffed, faded jeans were held snug on her hips by her thick black leather belt, and her white dress shirt had clearly been ironed only minutes ago. Her short dark hair was carefully combed, and I just knew she smelled of my favorite coconut lotion.

She looked handsome. The best part was the look in her eyes: Huge and brown and liquid, her eyes showed terror, resignation, heat, and adoration all at once. The way she looked at me made the hours of preparation worthwhile.

I motioned her silently toward me and pointed downward when she arrived. She knelt gracefully, her eyes full of emotion. I simply sat and looked at her for a moment, my heart full. Leaning forward, I kissed her cheek, gently, gently, and held her close, her head against my breast. Her eyes closed and she sighed. I was right—she did smell like coconut.

A minute or two of cuddling, then I couldn't restrain

myself any longer. I pulled her crisply ironed shirt off with impatient yanks at the buttons, and tugged her clean white tank over her head. Both ended up on the floor. Her eyes never wavered from my face.

I undid her belt and yanked it free of the belt loops in one long tug, and her eyes closed briefly, in pained anticipation. I watched her nipples grow hard.

"Whose sweet butch are you?" I whispered in her ear.

She pulled back to look me in the eye. "Yours. I'm yours."

"Take off the rest of your clothes."

She hopped to her feet and stripped, pulling her boots and socks off, then sliding her jeans and underwear down slim hips.

"I'm going to hurt you, Spike," I told her. "I'm going to hurt you a lot. I'm going to push you a little further than we've been before."

"Do whatever you want." She said it fervently. She said it like she meant it. I believed her.

I led my beloved to the center of the room, where I'd already hung two long chains from the ceiling, and stood her between them. Slowly, lovingly, I pulled suspension shackles around her wrists and clipped them just above her head. Then I wound a long leather strap around her waist, pulled it snug between her legs, and clipped it to the ends of the chains, keeping her almost on her toes.

"Try hard not to go off your feet." I spoke in her ear from behind, making her start. "If you do, this strap will dig in." I gave it a yank to demonstrate. She squeaked; I grinned.

I pulled a little table over beside Spike as she stood, nervously shifting from foot to foot within her bondage, and emptied my clip bag onto it with a clatter.

"This will be the easy part. Remember those little blue flowers?" I asked. "The ones you pull the petals off and say 'She loves me, she loves me not'?"

Spike started to smile.

"Well, we're gonna do it differently," I continued. "We're gonna say it with clothespins instead of flowers. And because we already know there's no chance in hell of me *not* loving you, you'll say 'She loves me' each time, meaning I, Elaine, love you. Got it, baby-cakes?"

"She loves me. Got it." Spike grinned.

I started with her back, and laid rows of clothespins across her shoulders, their tight-sprung jaws fierce on her soft skin. She took it well, repeating, "She loves me. She loves me. She loves me. She loves me." She spoke clearly and boldly, but her voice grew softer as more of the clips bit into her skin. When I reached the midpoint of her back, each clip brought a hiss and a growl: "She. Loves. Me."

I smiled and agreed, each time.

When I'd put clips all over her back, right to the bottom of her rib cage, I walked around to her front. Her smile was beatific. I kissed her and told her how very brave she was being, then I started putting rows of clips along her chest, down the sides of the ribs under her slightly raised arms.

"She loves me. She loves me..." Spike struggled for the words, but found them every time with every clip. Even when I switched my attentions to the softest skin on the backs of her thighs, placing clips as closely as I could find flesh to pinch up with them, she still didn't miss one whispered: "She loves me."

I was so proud of her. And I told her so, standing in front of her, whispering in her ear as she hung in chains, and nestled her face into my shoulder. And then I told her what I was going to do next. And asked her if she'd like a gag, so the neighbors didn't hear.

She nodded gratefully, her brown eyes soft. She was starting to fly a bit from the bite of the clothespins.

I gave her a soft flexible rubber ball to bite on, sliding it into her mouth on the heels of a kiss. Then I turned to my toy closet, and pulled out my whip.

"OK. My turn to speak." I said. "I love you for being so caring and so sweet with me." And I brought the whip, a heavy rubber flogger, whistling down across the clips on her back.

Spike screamed into her gag and shot forward against the bondage, swinging back as the first clips pattered to the carpet around our feet. She gave me a panicked, imploring glance over her shoulder before I spoke again.

"I love you for being so bright and smart and good to talk with," I told her. My whip struck her other shoulder; clips shot in the air, and Spike screamed wholeheartedly into her gag. I stroked her hair, looking into her eyes for a moment.

"I love you for the work you choose to do, and how it helps people." My whip struck again, downward across the clips above her breast, moving fast and sharp to keep the tails of the whip together. It made a wreckage of the careful rows of clips, and provoked another muffled scream and some anguished dancing from Spike.

We went through "I love you for being a bigger pervert than me, even," which brought a smirk around her gag, and "I love you for being the world's most fuckable human being," and "I love you because you make me laugh, even when I'm sad." Each sentence brought a whiplash, howl, and clatter of clips. I could see her pain becoming more and more intense, more than my sweet masochistic love usually enjoyed.

"I love you because you're such a soft-hearted, sensitive butch." I raised my whip, and Spike backed away on the tips of her toes as far as the chains would allow, tears starting at the corners of her eyes, her look pleading with me. I ducked down and with a quick flick of my wrist wrapped the whip around her thighs and pulled sharply.

With a pop, Spike's gag shot across the room, pushed by her full-throated shriek. Her legs pulled up to her body; she dangled, drawing breath to scream again. I dropped my whip and caught her up, taking some of her weight off the leather straps running between her legs. She was still covered with enough clips to make her hedgehoglike and hard to hold.

"Shh, my love. Don't make the neighbors call the cops."

I held her against me while she fought for breath and struggled with sobs. My own eyes welled with tears at what she was willing to do with me. When she'd recovered a bit, we kissed, long and deep. I told her again how wonderful I thought she was, and put her back on her feet. I picked up the whip again and turned to her.

"Do you need the gag again?"

"Oh, God. Say, why don't you take the rest off with something other than the whip? How about the riding crop? Oh, that would be much better," she said, already hopping worriedly. "Yeah, the riding crop."

"OK, I guess no gag." I smiled. "Hold in your screams, then."

"Hey! Wait!"

"I love you more than I can explain, and I'm lucky that you love me too. And you'd better never forget that," I said as she jigged anxiously from foot to foot, wide-eyed.

I hung my whip over my shoulder, and began plucking clips off as fast as I could grab them, saying: "I love you! I want you! I adore you! I appreciate you! I want to fuck you! I want you to fuck me! I love your cooking! I love playing like this with you! I like your taste in movies! I love spending time together! I love that we can read the same books! Your service means so much to me! I love you! Did I mention that I love you?"

Spike jumped and yelped with each tug and flare of pain, and laughed at the rate of my gabbling endearments. She spun around and around in her chains as I plucked clips from her shoulders, her ribs, over her breasts, and her thighs. As we came to the last few ferocious little clips, she, laughing, shouted: "I'll remember! I'll remember! You love me!"

And you know what? We ran out of clips long before I ran out of the reasons why I love her.

office 101: the student-teacher relationship | alissa overend

Picture yourself a professor sitting at your desk, deeply entrenched in Lacan's *Language of the Self*. You carry an arrogant air as you flip through the pages one by one, not wanting to be disturbed.

There's a knock at your office door, office number 101. You instruct the mystery knocker to "come in" in a firm, "this had better be important" tone. The door opens slowly. Picture me, a student: I attend lectures regularly and am generally a good student, but you've always sensed a slight edge in my attitude. This is my first time coming to your office because although I'm having some troubles reading Lacan, academic women often intimidate me. So I enter the room awkwardly—not sure what to do with the papers in my hand, the bag on my back, where to stand, or what to say. I have a mental list of questions, but I'm not sure where to begin.

You sit casually behind your desk with a faint smile, amused by my bumbling ways. You ask me to take a seat. This calms me until you ask, "Why have you come to see me?"

I freeze up. What if you think my questions are stupid? What if I'm wasting your time? "Um, I guess I'm just having a bit of trouble with Lacan...and, well—"

You roll your chair closer to your desk, take off your

glasses, perch forward, leaning your forearms on the desk, and say: "Lacan can be difficult. I still have problems understanding him sometimes." It soothes me to see this understanding, caring person beneath the often hard, distant professor we see in class. You reach across the table and touch my hand that is resting on your desk. "Not to worry," you continue. "We can go over some stuff right now."

My heart jumps; I like when you touch me. The sense of touch is a strange thing. Although you touch my hand, the sensation travels up my arm, across my shoulders, and instinctively finds its way to my nipples as they start to harden. I say to myself, *Don't turn red, don't turn red…quick answer the question.* So, as nonchalantly as possible, I reply, "Great."

You ask me to close the door. Without getting completely out of my chair, which is giving me a great deal of security at this moment, I reach behind and tap the door shut. As I turn back around, I swear I catch you looking at me—not as a teacher looking at a student, but as a sexually charged dyke eyeing someone she wants to engage with. Our eyes lock for a split second, and for that split second I'm no longer a shy, awkward student. I look directly into your eyes. We both feel the fire. But instead of acting on this feeling, I spend the next few seconds debating what the outcomes would be. Then, almost simultaneously, we shake ourselves out of the moment. Besides, you're the teacher and I'm the student; I'm not sure who's supposed to act first in these situations.

And so we proceed to discuss Lacan. It's funny—an intense, out-of-the-ordinary situation like this doesn't make me uncomfortable—it puts me at ease. My mind is now focused. I articulate my questions without choking. And best of all you are engaged, even fascinated.

I ask, as I start to piece together some Lacanian concepts, "So desire is everywhere, but it's neither detectable nor ever fully attainable?"

"Exactly! It's like trying to take hold of water running

through your fingers, but as soon as you go to reach for it, it disappears."

The mind is truly a multitasking marvel; I'm able to sit here and discuss various psychoanalytic concepts while at the same time thinking about your lips and hands. I wonder where your fingers have been, how many women they have fucked, when the last time you touched yourself was, and most of all, how good they would feel inside me. The door is shut; no one would ever know.

Your roll your chair from behind your desk closer to where I am sitting. We're almost touching but not quite. Right now the corner of your desk and the imaginary line I extend from it are the only boundaries between us. As we sit side-by-side, looking over one of Lacan's important passages, we infringe upon the invisible boundary with strategic and purposeful movements. Every so often our forearms, shoulders, thighs, or hands brush faintly. Our eyes lock while we talk.

I can tell you're as aroused as I am. There are short pauses in your speech, and after these hesitations you are slow to regain your train of thought. You're eloquent when you speak in class, but I can understand how swollen nipples and a wet cunt can distract.

I wonder, would you let me throw you up against your office walls, or on your desk, or over the chair you are sitting on? I want to fuck you all over this office.

Now, picture me naked on your desk—arms back, legs spread. I lick my fingers knowingly. You like watching me. The gentle rocking of my hips aches for your touch. I trace my hard, reddened nipples around each cold finger, slowly, tauntingly. What will you do to me? Will you tease me and make me groan? Will you let me spank you with a ruler you probably have tucked away in some drawer? I crave to thrust my hard, athletic boy body against yours—grinding and groaning fiercely until desire surrenders us and we release.

I pull you over to me and roughly unbutton your shirt.

You resist, clearing your throat and making excuses about impropriety. I spread my legs wider and roll your hard, pink nipples around my fingertips. You move into me, smiling as you brush you hand between my legs, rubbing me through the thin fabric of my pants.

I move one hand to my own nipple and tease us both in the same rhythm. My feet struggle to find the handles of your desk drawers and perch themselves there. Your hand presses harder; my feet flex. I let you know I want to feel your hand even harder by twisting your nipple until you lean into me. There's a noise outside the door and you jump, but your hand stay put. You find my hard clit and circle over it firmly. I hold my breath—

"*Jouissance*," you continue over my daydream, "as Lacan would say, is a type of pleasure beyond pleasure."

I leave your office with my clit throbbing and my labia swollen. We both continue our day as if nothing happened. I realize our session worked; I have finally understood many Lacanian concepts—although I'll be careful not to let on. What other reason would I have for revisiting office 101?

seoul train | diane kepler

I met her on the Sunday night Saemaul express out of Mokp'o. When I boarded at Taejon, the seat next to mine was vacant. I remember thinking what good fortune I had; it's a rare luxury to be able to spread across two whole train seats in a country as densely populated as South Korea.

Rare and, as it turned out, short-lived.

A girl got on at the very next stop. A ripple of annoyance claimed me at first, but that faded when I saw how gorgeous my seatmate was.

But no—wait. Saying it like that reduces what I felt to something based solely on looks, some animal reaction to her fawnlike legs and silky black hair. OK, sure, those things factored in, but they were only a small part of the whole package.

I first noticed her nails: pale, gleaming ovals, each with a swath of poppy red at the center. Then I caught her scent: a heady combination of soap and the musk of a single flower. That right-left combination of polish and perfume would have made me reel even if I hadn't seen her slender legs with ankles securely crossed. And that pin-striped miniskirt. And those leather knee boots. Then, when I glanced up and saw that her lips were not painted but just barely glossed, the twinge in my pussy became a spreading heat.

I observed her in furtive, sideways glances, like a swimmer taking breaths of air. I compared our forearms: mine sun-bronzed and dusted with a hundred fine hairs, hers paler and totally smooth. That got me thinking about running my hands over her skin, which was a dangerous road to be on. After all, any young woman who looked this hot probably had a boyfriend in Seoul, someone she'd date for eight months before he'd haltingly broach the subject of marriage (a proposal she'd squealingly accept, provided he'd meet with Omma and Appa's approval and come up with a rock the size of her navel). And when he'd ask her to sleep with him, she'd refuse on the pretext of being a traditional kind of girl. In reality it'd just be a delay tactic so she could slip away to Japan and get her hymen surgically repaired.

But just then I caught myself. Slagging the grapes because you couldn't have them was something Aesop had warned me about, so perhaps it was unfair pigeonholing Angel Eyes because she looked so straight. I could instead imagine this girl as my playmate, heck, even my partner. We'd live in a gorgeous Manhattan studio. If she was in the mood, she'd put her head on my shoulder or wear little rubber dresses. If I was in the mood I'd tie her up. She'd lick me until I came, and then I'd fuck her until she begged me to stop. We'd have friends over for parties, cook them amazing Korean food, and tell them stories about meeting on a train headed for Seoul.

The announcement for Suwon station jolted me out of my fantasy. I glanced around, startled. Then our eyes met.

It was a long glance. She dropped her gaze, but looked up again a moment later. It was the kind of thing a girl would do if she was trying to pick me up back home. Another crackle of energy sliced through me, leaping from pussy to nipple-tips. Was she flirting? Did she have any clue about what this leather jacket meant? These freedom rings?

"May I introduce myself?" she said.

I smiled agreeably while exulting inside. This was too easy!

"My name is Son Nya Kim. I am from Seoul. I am Doksung Women's University student. My major is language. My family is five: father, mother, me, younger sister, younger brother." She rattled this off with a decided formality, sounding like a schoolgirl giving a speech. It was a tune I'd heard before. Not a submissive's siren song, merely the opening motif of the *Let's Practice Our English* concerto. Inwardly I sighed.

"May I ask you name?" she probed.

"Terri," I said with typical Western informality. "Sorry, Kim is your family name, right? Kim Son Nya?"

"Yes," she said, and brightened, no doubt pleased that this foreigner wasn't as culturally dense as some. "What are you doing?"

I blinked at her. "I'm taking the train to Seoul."

"No, sorry." Her brow creased by thought-lines, which made her look even more attractive. "I mean... What do you do?"

"Oh!" I grinned. "I'm a photographer. I take pictures for travel magazines. Here." Out of the bag at my feet, I pulled one of the Nikon bodies I always keep at the ready, the one with the 60-mm macro lens attached. Leaning back, I got her vaguely centered and squeezed off a shot before she had time to react.

Her response was not the predictable "oh my hair's a mess" noise. Instead she eyed the camera with interest and asked to see it. I put the Nikon on full auto and then handed it over. Right away, she composed a shot of me against the train window. "*Chee-juh!*" she called merrily. I'd learned some time ago that there's no "z" sound in the Korean language.

When she'd captured my best wry grin, I could tell the ice had been broken. We chatted with increasing friendliness as the train slid along its silver rails.

"*Onni*, you so pretty," Son Nya said, using the familiar

Korean word for older sister. She cast a glance at my blond hair. "Like Meg Ryan."

I refrained from saying that Ryan couldn't hold a candle to Son Nya, but only because it was such a cliché. I just complimented her in subtler ways until we hit Seoul station, where I got the unexpected pleasure of feeling her small, round ass against my thighs as the mob behind us pushed and shoved its way off the train. But when we hit the platform, I realized the bag with my clothes was still on board. By the time I'd retrieved it, Son Nya was gone.

I cursed myself a hundred times, but then realized it was moot anyway—Koreans don't admit there are such things as lesbians, much less lesbians with a leather scene. I hadn't heard of a single party or club since I'd been here.

Thus I let the idea of Son Nya slip away. The whole thing would have dissolved into one of the great what-ifs of my life, that is, if she hadn't been waiting for me at the top of the stairs. "*Onni*, you have many bag. I help carry."

I was pleased and surprised, but then remembered not to be. Most Koreans had an almost stubborn politeness about them. It was one of the things that made working here so pleasant.

"Where are you going?" she asked, as we navigated the olive-skinned sea.

Desperation or possibly hope gave me a sudden idea. "Son Nya, you live in Seoul, right?"

"Yes." She looked at me earnestly.

"You must know the big shopping district, Myeong-dong?"

"Of course. It is very popular place."

"I have to take some photos there, and if you could spare some time, I'd really appreciate it if you could tell me about some of the really good hangouts—good places to sit with friends and talk."

She nodded exuberantly. "I show you."

Perfect.

So that's how it went. We stowed our extra things in lockers and hopped the subway downtown. Chonggak station was just two stops away on the Red Line, but no way was I telling Son Nya I knew this.

At first I just shot pictures of the vendors working and the hipsters with their dyed hair and platform shoes. But Son Nya distracted me. She'd changed clothes at the station and was looking quite edible in her beret, sneakers, cargo pants, and a red and blue baby tee with a big number 5 on it. The shirt was tight and showed off her small breasts. I felt a ripple of pleasure as I imagined tonguing her sweet brown nipples into erection.

"Son Nya," I said in a voice as low as the traffic would allow, "Go stand over there." She looked at me quizzically for a moment but then obeyed—a good sign.

"OK, now turn toward that window. Look toward my reflection in the glass. No, don't smile. That's good. Yes."

I took a beautiful shot of her with the Leica: wide aperture, soft focus. It's now one of a series on my bedroom wall at home.

"Turn halfway toward me. Look over my right shoulder. Further right. Serious face. Hold that. Yes."

I talked her through a few more shots. It was amazing to see how well she obeyed orders. My panties were wet; I wanted so much to just push her up against the side of a building and claim those rosebud lips. But I reined in the urge, instead steering her toward a video parlor. It was typically seedy—an office space partitioned off into a warren of little cubbyholes, each with a ratty old love seat and a big-screen TV. Technically these places were illegal, but given their problems in the North, the government had bigger things to worry about.

Son Nya agreed that it'd be good to sit down after all that walking, and made no further comment. But then again, why should she? Over here same-sex friends watched videos together all the time.

The film I selected was *Bound*—a brilliant take on butch-meets-femme for Son Nya's benefit.

Some of my playmates swear I'm telepathic, but I'm not. I just pay strict attention to every motion and glance and breath a woman makes. This watchfulness allowed me to see two critical shifts in my Son Nya's awareness: first, when she understood the film's subtext, and second, when she understood why I'd brought her here. Both realizations came sooner than I'd hoped. Clever girl.

We'd been shoulder to shoulder since the beginning. Again, nothing unusual in this part of the world. But when I felt her second instant of comprehension, I turned toward her and dipped my head until it was resting near the crown of hers. I gathered a handful of her jasmine-scented hair and pressed it to my lips.

I nuzzled the side of her neck, waiting to see if she'd resist or pull away. She did neither, so I kissed the soft spot at the juncture of her neck and shoulder. She reached over to put her hand on my arm, but there was no force behind it. Instead, she relaxed and let her head roll to the side. Yes!

My kisses turned into licks. I traced a moist line down her neck and then blew on it. She shivered, just as I'd hoped. Then I moved in. My kisses grew more insistent, and soft murmurs escaped her. When my kisses changed to nips, her hand clutched my forearm, beautiful painted nails digging in. That got me so turned on, I pulled the neck of her T-shirt down and began to feast on the side of her neck. Son Nya gave me an unambiguous hiss of pleasure.

I leaned away for an instant to mute the TV. Then I turned back to have a look at my prize. She was reclining passively on the tattered couch, her eyes two ebony pools. I gave her my most wicked smile, letting her know she was in for something different.

I slid a hand under her baby tee and caressed her soft, flat belly. Even that gentle contact with her skin made my throbbing clit swell up and press itself against the seam of my jeans. I wanted to feel her mouth against it.

But there were other things to take care of first. Most importantly, I had to see how far her obedience extended, so I folded her shirt back to expose her stomach and then raked my nails across it. I watched a quartet of red lines come up. She moaned, causing little fireworks go off inside me.

I rearranged Son Nya until she was in the middle of the couch, her arms spread out across the sloping backrest, her legs supported by the padded bench that was serving as an ottoman. "I want to see your body, " I whispered.

Son Nya whimpered but didn't reply.

"Gonna show me those titties, that puss?" I touched each part as I named it to minimize any confusion.

Again, no reaction but for a soft sound, like the cooing of a dove.

"Come on. Show me."

Avoiding my eyes, she tugged up her shirt until her bra was showing. Cotton, with little blue flowers. I traced each nipple with a careful finger. With a girl who knew the game, I would have been far more direct, maybe pinching them until she arched her back and wailed. I had to be careful with this one, though.

"Show me all of yourself, Son Nya."

By now she had her eyes closed and her head turned to the side. It was a familiar pose. Avoidance. But her cunt, where it rested against my knee, was warm. She wanted this. I waited patiently until she'd reached behind her back, unhooked the bra, and pushed that up too.

Her breasts were of a kind I hadn't seen since high school: small, conical, and relentlessly perky. Her nipples were already hard. I slipped one into my mouth and swirled my tongue around it while I tugged then pinched the other. After awhile I switched sides, tonguing the now swollen nipple and pinching the moist one good and hard.

"Do you like that, Son Nya?"

Clearly she did, but I wanted to hear her say it. I wanted her to open her eyes, meet my gaze, and acknowledge it. I grabbed a fistful of that shimmering hair and gently turned her to face me.

When she opened her eyes, I just about fell over. Her gaze was so intense that I fished the Leica point-and-shoot out of my jacket to make this a Kodak moment too. I still have that photo. It's grainy and a little blurred, but it suits the moment exactly. Whenever I look at it, I can see how wide and dark her eyes were, how soft her barely parted lips. And although it's just a head-and-shoulders shot, I can see the wrinkles in her shirt where she's pulled it up.

After that, it was surprisingly easy to get Son Nya out of her pants. I just told her to strip and then watched as she lifted her hips to inch the tan denim down. My fingers followed the path of her jeans. I cupped her mound in the palm of my hand, pressing the lips together as I moved my hand in small, circular motions. When Son Nya canted her hips toward me I knew she was ready for more, so I let my middle finger get into the wet groove. I slid it back and forth for a while, building up a rhythm, letting her relax into the hollow of my shoulder before suddenly plunging it into her hole, right up to the last knuckle.

Son Nya gasped. I covered her mouth with mine and swallowed that delightful sound. I thought of binding her and filling her with my shiny black dildo.

And as if the presence of Son Nya and my own crazed imaginings weren't enough to get me hot, somebody was watching porn in the next cubicle. It galvanized me; I broke off the kiss and got to work on her clit. I backed off when I felt her near the edge. It was time to push things a little further.

I lifted my head from her pussy and stood up. With my hands on her upper arms and my face in shadow, I knew I appeared rather menacing. "What a nasty little girl," I accused, holding her away from me. "Making all that noise like you were in a sex movie. Nice girls don't do that."

For an instant, Son Nya showed me the shadow of a smile. She knew it was a game. Somehow she knew.

"*Onni*—"

"Not another single word," I hissed. Her distress was a joy. "Are you sorry? Move your head like this if you are."

Trembling, she nodded. But it wasn't the gesture that mattered, it was the understanding. She knew her power and then gave it to me. I didn't have to search; it was there.

"I'm happy that you want to be good," I continued, "but we have to make sure you get there. Do you know how we do that?"

Wordlessly, we moved into place, me on the couch and her face-down across my lap. I positively ached to take a picture of the inviting globes of her ass, but it would have ruined the moment. Instead I caressed her with my hand. Then I brought it down, grateful for the overpowering sound from the video next door.

God, what a feeling to have her wriggle against my thighs. And that cry she gave—exquisite! I followed up with three strokes, a pause, then an even six. Soon I lost count. Then I lost myself in the rhythm, mesmerized by the way she hollowed out her back and pushed herself toward me.

Finally, I just couldn't take it anymore. I pushed her up and knelt on the couch with one hand in her hair and the other tearing at my belt, my zipper. I pushed everything off and then brought her forward: "Lick it. Put your...ah-h-h..."

She was a complete natural, working away at my clit like it was wired to both of our minds. Her gleaming hair swayed and bobbed in the blue TV light. Behind it all was the thought of her ass glowing a most enticing pink. I wished there were mirrors so I could see all of us at once.

I came in heart-stopping, breath-stealing waves. Right after the most intense sensations had ebbed, I pulled her up beside me. I got a hand down into her summery petal-place and opened her. It was all so easy, so smooth. She'd relaxed a little and now I could get three fingers up into her. Her pussy squeezed them into a triangle, two in back and one in front, which I used to stroke her G spot. She flushed and her breathing quickened. I fucked her harder and every so often brushed her burgeoning clit with my thumb.

The last moments were magical. She was all moans and sighs and black-fringed eyes, helpless in a sea of pleasure. White-fisted, she groaned, "Oh, Jesus," and spilled her desire into my hand.

I didn't so much lie back on the couch as melt into it. Son Nya reclined against me with her head on my shoulder and her hand enfolding the one I'd used to get her off. She kissed each fingertip. A feeling of peace spread over me. I marveled yet again at her perfection and at my luck.

But I had a nagging thought. I must have lay there for 10 minutes before I figured it out. "Jesus," she'd said. With a "z" sound.

My eyes opened. "Son Nya?"

"Mm?"

"Feel like telling me where you're really from?"

Her eyes fluttered open. She pursed her lips, twisted them, and then gazed at me levelly. At last, a mischievous grin appeared. "From Seoul." She blushed, looked down, and then met my eyes again. "But my family moved to Vancouver when I was 8."

My eyes widened. I was still so drugged with pleasure that it took me a moment to respond to her perfect diction, her complete lack of an accent. "You're...you..."

"But I am going to school here. To Doksung."

I felt dizzy. Faint. So I asked a lame question. "What's...your major?"

"I'm about to get my Masters in linguistics."

That was my cue to start laughing, which I did, first in broken chuckles, like an old car starting up, and then in as full comprehension dawned, in long unrestrained roars.

It still cracks me up. Even now, when we go out to fetish parties and people ask how I met the love of my life, I can't keep a straight face.

sadie's bar | vickie l. spray

I hadn't been in a bar in years, but Jessie had just broken up with her girlfriend and wanted to celebrate. We were on the road to a writer's conference in Chicago, so we checked in the lesbian directory and found Sadie's Bar: "Dancing, pool tables, and free surprises for first-time visitors."

"Oh, fun! I wonder what the surprises are."

We arrived ten minutes later. The bar gave me the sensation of being in the presence of an old lover—it was familiar but no longer a part of me. I squinted my eyes to adjust to the darkness. White sheer fabric covered the ceiling, creating a canopy over the front room. The fabric undulated as the outdoor breeze passed under them. I felt certain I smelled baby oil.

I scanned the empty front room, then the pool room in back. There were two women standing in a corner facing each other, their pool cues held between them like stiff reeds. A few other women could be seen sitting at the tables to the right of the pool room. Everyone intently watched us walk to the bar. When I looked at the pool table I saw that the balls had been arranged like a stick figure with the legs open wide.

Jessie and I ordered our drinks from a big woman with short black hair made lighter by patches of gray. Her hand, moist from her work, touched the back of mine as I reached for my glass; her smile confirmed the touch to be intentional. She looked over at the group of women I had seen watching us and subtly nodded. I looked at Jessie, who raised one arched shaped eyebrow and grinned with a shrug.

"Looks like you could get a kiss or two tonight if you wanted it," she said, smiling at me mischievously.

"Or I could just watch you," I said. She looked good tonight. Creases around her bright brown eyes wrinkled as she smiled. The blond hair coloring we had put on her hair brought out the light blond of her eyelashes and eyebrows. She looked happy and open—a woman not afraid to have fun.

More women entered the bar. They jostled each other and walked with an enthusiastic swagger toward the pool tables and dance floor. Women I had not previously noticed moved from one table to another, making the rounds. Many of them were whispering and talking excitedly.

My attention was abruptly riveted to a woman who, without any inhibition, was staring at Jessie. Her lips were set in a slight smile like a half-opened seashell. She had long dark hair, wore a black open-backed dress, and had around her neck a magnificent piece of brightly colored African jewelry. I recognized her as one of the women who had been going table to table, talking with all the patrons.

"Jessie," I whispered.

"I see her," she whispered. She and the woman stared at one another. Jessie's brown eyes were steady; her body was immobile.

At that moment everyone at the table with the woman in the black dress leaned in to her words, then glanced in our direction. Some laughed. I looked again at Jessie. She continued to stare, undaunted by the new atmosphere at the table. There was more talk and more inquisitive stares in our direction; they were plotting something. While I tried to look disinterested and tried twice more to get Jessie's attention away from the table, a concentration of energy gathered in the room. Those who had been playing pool stopped. Those who had been dancing ceased moving. Everyone turned toward the table where the woman in black sat.

Suddenly, the women at the table moved toward us. The sound of chairs pushing back filled the room. They approached in a choreographed sway of agreement. There were six of them. My mind convulsed half sentences of possible explanations, but none made any sense.

I wondered if I should be afraid. Their faces were set with some purpose but lacked any look of malice, and the approach of their bodies was without intimidation. I glanced at Jessie, and to my amazement she was smiling.

The woman in black was the first to arrive. She smiled at Jessie, openly searching her for signs of fear. Seeing none, she moved to the front of her. She turned Jessie's body and slipped between her spread legs in one solid smooth movement. The five other women made a half circle around Jessie, leaving me out of their intentions but still within view. Jessie looked at the woman in black and at the women who had surrounded her as though they had all been friends and now were about to share a secret.

Two women, one on either side of her, reached for Jessie's arms and pinned them against the top of the bar counter. I remembered the spread-eagle stick figure on the pool table and felt the pores on my skin open to the tense concentration of the room.

Jessie couldn't move. A tall white woman wearing a loose red skirt stepped to the right of her leg, reached over, and began to unbutton Jessie's shirt. The roundness of Jessie's breast pushed against the fabric.

I suddenly felt myself measure the distance between Jessie's nipple and my tongue, as the women leaned in toward the center of the circle where Jessie's hard nipple waited. We stood still wondering what the woman in black would do next. I never wanted to fuck someone so much in my life. I made a slight move but the second I did, three women, one of them the tanned bartender, surrounded me. Their purpose was clear: I was not the one to have Jessie.

A woman whose skin shone like coal beneath the moon stepped to the left side of Jessie. She wore a pin-striped suit; her short kinky hair was slicked back. She looked at the woman in black obtaining, it seemed, permission to continue. On getting it, she kissed the curve of Jessie's ear and her temple. Jessie closed her eyes. The woman who had unbuttoned Jessie's shirt put her hand on Jessie's stomach and nudged the remaining portion of the shirt away from her body so both of Jessie's breasts were available.

The pin-striped woman moved her lips to Jessie's. She wore two gold rings that glistened like yellow strobe lights, first on Jessie's face then her stomach and breast. Jessie arched her body forward but her arms were still pinned by the women beside her.

The women behind me leaned in closer, and I felt two sets of breast press against me. I looked at the woman in the black dress who'd been standing still between Jessie's legs as if watching a fascinating show put on just for her. She glanced up at me and smiled.

The hand with the gold ring moved slow circles on Jessie's breast. A moan came from Jessie's throat. The hand then slipped under Jessie's belt. My pelvis instinctively pushed forward as I watched the bulge in Jessie's pants spread her legs wide.

The woman who had unbuttoned Jessie's shirt leaned over and covered Jessie's left nipple with her lips. I felt the two women behind me touching themselves. The woman in black stepped farther between Jessie's legs and whispered in her ear. Jessie nodded. The two women behind me stepped back and the women pinning Jessie's arms moved away.

The skin around Jessie's lips was pinkish, smeared with lipstick. Her hair was darkened with sweat. Jessie lifted herself from the barstool with the help of the women flanking her. She didn't seem to notice me as she passed by. I again attempted to move toward her and again I was blocked. This time the bartender smiled when I looked into her eyes. I knew she wanted me.

Jessie and the woman in black moved within a sea of women to the backroom with the pool tables. My body-guards, as I was beginning to think of them, stood beside me until everyone had passed.

"Well, girls," I said with a bravado I didn't feel, "what's going to happen next?"

No one answered.

The bartender lifted my arm, indicating that I was to get up. We moved, me still between their bodies, toward the backroom.

There was a crowd of onlookers surrounding one of the pool tables. The low sound of drumming began as the women tapped on the pool tables in unison. I felt each vibration while I was lead to the back wall and placed on a chair that was about hip height with no back.

I didn't like this arrangement. I wanted to know where Jessie and the woman in black were; I wanted to know what was going to happen. Before I could protest, however, I saw the woman in black step out from the crowd at the far end of the pool table. To my amazement, she turned and looked at me.

Her eyes were like a book I had wanted to read but didn't have the courage to open. She continued to stare at me even as two women came up behind her and presented a belted dildo harness. Her smile widened as they fixed the harness with a dildo and strapped it around her hips. They pulled the middle strap up between her legs, bunching the material of her dress up to her thighs, where I could see the lighter edge of her nylon stockings. Someone stepped in front of her and in one quick solid motion covered the dildo with a condom.

The overwhelming physical yearning I'd felt earlier returned in full measure. I didn't want her to see this, but I know she did. She then nodded toward the women encircling the table. They parted from the table and presented me with a clear view of Jessie stretched out naked in the center of a pool table, her arms above her head, her legs spread. The light of the candles cast reaching shadows across her body; her face was turned toward the ceiling. She lay there as if she had been forcefully instructed to be still.

As the woman in black climbed onto the table, my three friendly bodyguards changed positions. The bartender moved behind me while the other two stepped a few feet out on either side behind me. I again felt their breasts against my body. I also felt their heightened lust as they pressed themselves closer to me. The bartender, her strong arms feeling powerful against me, slipped her hands beneath my shirt.

The woman in black covered Jessie's body with her own. My nipples hardened. The black dress fell over Jessie's white body like an eclipse. The woman kissed Jessie's lips and began to move against her with a circular rhythm. My breast yielded to cupped hands that squeezed roughly with mounting impatience. I fell back onto the bartender's breast. I arched my back as I watched Jessie's hips move against the hips of the woman in black. The woman raised her upper body up from Jessie and I saw Jessie's nipple covered in red lipstick. Her breast moved like swaying islands as the woman churned her body into Jessie's.

The woman to my right stepped up and turned toward me. She reached down and lifted my shirt over my head. Her mouth was on my breast before my shirt was completely removed. The woman on the other side of me lowered her head onto my other breast.

Through the sliver of my barely opened eyes, I saw the woman in black sitting up on her knees between Jessie's spread legs. Some type of oil had been spread on Jessie's body. The curves of her hips, thighs, stomach, and breasts glistened in the light of the candles. The woman in black smiled as she steadied the dildo with one hand. She gently entered Jessie, who pitched her chest upward, turned her head to the side, and bit her lower lip.

I spread my legs wider as the woman began to slowly pump my friend. Jessie clung to the woman. I stretched my fingers across both women's heads as they continued to suck my breasts.

The bartender nudged me forward and gently moved away from the wall. She came around the other women and stood in front of me, then undid my belt. I lifted my body as she pulled my pants over my hips. She surprised me by reaching down to undo her belt. When her pants dropped, I saw the dildo.

The bartender slipped on a condom and stepped between my legs. I wrapped a leg around her and urged the hardness inside me, feeling its length slide into me. The women on my breasts sucked in rhythm, each with an arm around my back. We all rocked together with the slow thrusts.

She watched me as she slid more of the dildo inside. My breaths shortened. The women at my breasts moved behind me again; I felt them each time the bartender pushed her hips against me. She grabbed either side of my hips and drew me to her. My hips banged against the hardness of the chair each time she entered me.

Jessie's hips lifted to meet the downward stroke of the woman's hips. The harness strap strained with each push. She moaned loudly. My thighs met the quickened movement of the dildo. Our bodies both slammed into the hardness of the dildos while our half-opened eyes looked into the soft faces of women giving and taking pleasure. Our breasts shook with each movement. Back and forth, in and out, we clasped on to these strangers and screamed.

"More?" they asked.

"Yes," we said.

"Harder?" they asked.

"Yes!" we screamed.

Jessie's head rolled from side to side. She clawed at the woman's back. I heard the sound of wet skin slapping wet skin. I smelled my wetness mixed with the heat of our body's friction. I heard Jessie crying, "Yes...Yes...Yes!" as she started to climax.

I arched my back as a glowing ball of pleasure rolled inside my hips, thighs, and legs. My body was liquid poured over the edges of the chair, down onto the floor. One of the woman behind me reached around and circled my hard clit until I was shaking and panting. Finally, I pressed forward, grabbing on to her hand so she wouldn't stop, and came with a loud cry.

No one moved for quite a while, then one by one the women standing around the table walked slowly from the room as if they had been a dream. The women beside me eased toward the door as my valiant bartender kissed me on the lips and walked away.

The woman in black raised herself from the table. She undid the harness from around her waist, put it on a nearby table, and straightened out her wrinkled dress. She kissed Jessie then walked out the door with one sideways glance in my direction.

The place was empty except for a clean-up person who was wiping up behind the bar. She softly whistled a ballad I recognized. The absurdity of the whistled tune within the foggy memory of what had just happened collided with my diminished sense of propriety. A laugh exploded from my tired ribs.

Jessie, still naked, still spread out on an oil soaked pool table, also began laughing. I stood up to go to her, tripped over my pants, which were still down at my ankles, stumbled as I raised them up to my hips, and barely made it to the pool table. I fell onto the table and wrapped myself around my friend, laughing harder.

the things you do for love |
maria v. ciletti

I hate camping. I find nothing attractive about sleeping in a tent on the hard ground out in the middle of nowhere. I'm just not the outdoorsy type. Unfortunately Regan is, and since I don't want to be stuck home alone on this Fourth of July weekend, I agreed to go camping in the Pennsylvania mountains. The things you do for love.

We packed up Regan's SUV with her camping equipment then headed for the KOA campground in Cook's Forest. The four-hour drive was long and oppressively hot, especially since Nature Girl refused to turn on the air conditioning in the car. "The fresh air's good for you," she said, breathing in deeply as I peeled off my sweat soaked T-shirt.

We arrived at the campground entrance and took our place behind an extremely long line of cars, trucks, and SUVs. "Wow, looks like everyone had the same idea for this weekend," I said, fanning myself with the map.

"Yeah, I hope all the good campsites aren't taken," she answered as she cheerfully drummed her fingers on the steering wheel in time with a Tracy Chapman tune coming from the CD player.

A mutual friend had introduced Regan and me six weeks before at the only gay bar in Youngstown, Ohio. I had just gotten off work at the hospital and stopped in for a quick drink when Carol, the respiratory therapist I worked with, dragged Regan over and introduced us.

Regan was a nursing student finishing up her last clinical rotation at our hospital before graduating; I'm a staff nurse from the urology floor, so naturally Karen thought we'd have a lot in common. She was right. One drink turned into two, then three, until finally Regan and I closed the bar. A week later we had dinner at her place—a meal that lasted well into the next morning. We've been inseparable ever since.

Our car inched along in the blazing July sun. Finally, we reached the park ranger's booth. "Reservation number please," he asked.

"Reservation? I didn't know we needed a reservation," Regan said.

"Yes, miss, you do. This is a holiday weekend. Everyone needs a reservation. If you don't have one, I'll have to ask you to turn around."

"Don't you have anything available?" she asked sweetly, turning on the same charm that got me where I am today. "Any...ah...last-minute cancellations?" She flashed her sexy smile at the weary-eyed Ranger.

"No, miss, I'm sorry. We're booked solid. If you don't have a reservation, I'll have to ask you to turn around."

Regan jerked the car around and we sped off. It was much easier getting out of the campground then getting into it.

"Now what are we going to do?" she asked, sullen. "Our weekend is ruined."

"Maybe there's a hotel or a bed and breakfast some where around here," I said.

"It's Fourth of July weekend. We'll never find anything on this short notice."

We traveled down the winding mountain road for about five miles and came across a visitors information center. "Pull in here," I said.

"Ah-h-h...air conditioning," I murmured as I pushed

open the heavy glass door and the cool air washed over me. I walked over to a huge oak paneled wall containing pamphlets for all the attractions in the Cook's Forest area, selected a few, pulled out my cell phone, and began calling.

Nine calls and $23.50 in roaming charges later, we still had nowhere to stay. The last pamphlet was for a "quaint" bed and breakfast that was only 2.2 miles from the visitors center. I dialed the number.

"I know this is late notice, but do you have anything available for this weekend?" I asked the clerk, who had finally picked up after the fifth ring.

I heard the clicking of computer keys on the other end of the phone. Long silence, then more clicking. "The only thing we have available this weekend is the Honeymoon Suite," she said.

"All that's left is the Honeymoon Suite." I mouthed over to Regan. She shrugged her shoulders in reply.

"How much for one night?" I asked.

"$480.00."

"$480.00! My God! I don't want to buy the place; I just want to stay the night!"

The silence on the other end of the phone made it clear this woman didn't appreciate my sense of humor. "It's a holiday weekend," she reminded me sternly. "However, the price does include a bottle of champagne, surf and turf dinner for two, and a gourmet breakfast served in your room."

"OK, we'll take it," I said.

Regan's eyes grew wode. "That's too expensive! What if the place is a dump? That's a lot of money to spend on a dump."

"I know, but what other options do we have? Do you want to sleep in the car all night?"

Regan shook her head and sighed.

We drove 2.2 miles to the rustic inn nestled in a forest paradise. The inn looked more like a Tuscan villa than a Pennsylvanian B&B. *Quaint* was not the word for this place; it was awesome.

Regan and I grabbed our backpacks out of the backseat and headed up the cobblestone walkway.

"Hi. I just spoke to someone on the phone. We're here for the Honeymoon Suite," I said as I approached the antique oak reception desk, pulling my Visa from my back pocket.

The desk clerk raised one eyebrow looking up at me in my faded RELAY FOR LIFE shirt and denim cutoffs, then over at Regan who was wearing cargo shorts, a Melissa Etheridge T-shirt, tan leather hiking boots, and a red bandanna tied around her head. Obviously we were underdressed for this place.

The clerk cleared her throat: "There's only one bed in the Honeymoon Suite. I can have a roll-a-way brought up if you like."

I smiled, trying to contain my amusement and looked over at Regan who avoided my gaze by feigning interest in an advertisement for a trout-fishing contest.

"No...that won't be necessary," I said.

The clerk finished up her paperwork and slid the key toward me across the top of the antique desk. "You can bring your...ah...luggage in through the main entrance. Your room is the last door on the right down this hall," she instructed, forcing a demure smile as she cautiously peered over the desk at our backpacks on the floor.

Regan and I headed down the richly paneled hallway. I put the key in the door and turned the gold knob. Plush maroon carpet led from the foyer into a huge bedroom where it spilled down to a sunken sitting area complete with a wet bar and entertainment center. Gold laminated mirrors gleamed from each wall. A white marble Jacuzzi waited in the far corner next to a walk-in shower that had not one but four gold-plated showerheads. Paradise.

Regan and I stood in the bedroom. Two huge crystal vases overflowing with white roses and lilacs flanked the antique oak four-poster bed; a silver ice bucket cradling a magnum of champagne sat on the oak nightstand.

"Well, it's not the great outdoors, but I guess it'll do...right?" I asked, while Regan shrug off her backpack and walked over to the bed. She kicked off her hiking boots and climbed up on to the bed.

She looked over at me and smiled a slow seductive smile. Slowly she peeled off her T-shirt, revealing beautiful tan breasts. I stood mesmerized, watching her as she slithered her taut body against the silk bedspread. She shimmied out of her cargo shorts and was now completely naked, except for the red bandanna, and lying face down on top of the bed.

"My back's a little stiff from all that driving," she said as she wiggled on the bed. "Would you..." I immediately dropped my backpack, kicked off my Doc Martens, and joined her.

I massaged her back slowly, savoring the feel of her supple warm skin under my fingers. She purred under my touch. I climbed on top of her, straddled her hips, and continued to rub her shoulders and back, kneading and massaging her smooth muscles. The exercise warmed me, so I pulled my T-shirt over my head and tossed it onto the floor. A low moan escaped her lips when I leaned forward, my erect nipples grazing her skin as I slowly slid my naked breasts down the length off her strong back.

I continued to massage her lower back and buttocks. When I reached her thighs, she spread her legs and gave me a nice view, but more importantly, better access to the part of her that craved attention the most.

I removed the rest of my clothes and stretched out on top of her, pinning her to the bed, feeling her soft, warm body under mine. I kissed her neck and shoulders, then slowly trailed my tongue down her spine. She shivered.

I nuzzled the soft cheeks of her butt and rubbed my face against her smooth legs. I kissed and licked the back of her knees and she moaned again in sweet agony. "You're driving me crazy," she said, heaving a sigh.

Her tormented moan was a heady invitation, so I continued my assent, alternately kissing and caressing her silky inner thighs. She squirmed in frustration, lifting her hips off the bed to give me direction. Her pussy was now inches from my face. I blew a soft stream of air onto her clit and her body trembled.

"Please..." Regan begged, both hands now clutching the bed spread. I playfully blew on her again until she squirmed.

Finally now positioned beneath her, I plunged in. Regan's swollen clit was hard against my tongue. She buried her face into the mattress, stifling her moans of pleasure. Her clit bounced on my tongue as I licked her until her body began to vibrate. Now I moved slowly on her aching spot until she was moaning, holding her breath in anticipation.

Moments later, Regan's legs buckled and she came. Her hair was damp with sweat; her skin glowed pink with orgasmic flush. I pulled her to me and held her close, stroking her hair as we both drifted off into a peaceful, contented sleep.

When I awoke from my little nap, I couldn't move my arms. Quite a bit of time had passed, obviously; the shadows in the room were long now. Regan was still naked, sitting at the foot of the bed. I tried again to get up, but couldn't.

"What are you doing?" I asked, nervousness creeping into my voice.

"You really made me wait to come. Turnaround is fair play," she said, her voice low and smooth.

Regan had bound my wrists to the bedposts with two bungee cords from her backpack, rendering me helpless. She hovered over me, both arms stiff and straight, supporting her weight on either side of me. Hard nipples brushed against hard nipples. She lowered her face to mine and kissed me, sweetly at first and then hard. Her tongue ravaged my mouth, setting my body on fire.

She broke our kiss and moved her hot mouth over my left breast. She sucked hard then swirled her tongue around my taut nipple. She kissed and licked one breast while fondling the other. Both nipples ached, and I knew I could come soon.

Regan pulled herself up, slid forward, and straddled my chest, her pussy inches from my face. I breathed in her musky scent. "You want some of this, don't you?" she whispered huskily, sliding her fingers through her glossy black pubic hair.

I nodded, mesmerized. I wanted to taste her again; no, I *ached* to taste her, but Regan cold-heartedly pulled away.

"Uh-uh-uh, you're gonna wait, just like you made me wait," she said sternly. My clit throbbed as Regan rocked back and forth on my chest; I felt the warm wetness of her pussy.

"Oh-h-h, my cunt is so wet," she whispered as she reached down and caressed herself. When she slid one finger inside her pussy I felt my own pussy contract.

"You looks so good..." I moaned, unconsciously licking my lips.

Regan slid two, then three slick fingers inside herself while she stroked her engorged clit with her other hand. Passion pounded through my body, powerless to move as I watched her. Regan's pace quickened; her breathing came in short forced bursts.

"Yes, oh, yes," she gasped, hips bucking wildly on my chest. She came hard and loud; for a moment I was worried the people in the next room might hear her.

She rolled off me and curled up, resting her head on my shoulder. Lazily she traced my nipples with her fingertips.

My body hummed under her touch. I was in agony.

Regan raised herself up on one elbow, a dreamy, satisfied smile across her face. "How are ya doin'?" she asked in a low lazy drawl while she teased my tortured nipple again.

"I'm dyin' here," I answered, my voice raspy. I wriggled on the bed and pulled at my restraints.

"Looks like you could use a little help," she said. "I'll see what I can do."

Regan reached up and untied her red bandanna, removing it from her shiny cap of black hair. "I want you to really feel everything I'm going to do to you." She snapped the bandanna between her hands, placed it over my eyes, and tied it around my head.

My heart pounded. The room went dark and deathly quiet. Now that I couldn't see Regan, every movement she made seemed amplified. I tugged at the bungee cords.

She reached down between my legs and slid one finger inside me. She moaned with approval and quickly withdrew her finger. She smeared my salty juices across my lips, bent down and kissed me, ravishing my mouth. I kissed her back until she pulled away quickly, leaving me weak.

The mattress coils creaked as Regan moved off the bed. A few seconds later I heard the rustling of foil and then *pop*!

"How about some champagne?" she asked as she returned to my side. "You look like you could use a little cooling off."

Suddenly, cold wetness splashed over my breasts. Regan slowly lapped the fizzing liquid from my body. I closed my eyes behind the bandanna, taking in all the exquisite sensations: the titillating coldness of the champagne, the warm softness of Regan's tongue.

I felt her body shift on the bed again as she positioned herself, now between my legs; finally, I would get some relief.

"My, my...you are wet," she whispered.

I squirmed in response.

Regan placed the opening of the champagne bottle at the entrance of my vagina, its cold firmness sending me jolting off the bed. "You like that? You want something hard in there, don't you?" she breathed.

She traced her slick finger along my swollen outer lips. I wiggled around, trying to rub my pussy against her finger, the champagne bottle, *anything* to feel relief, but again Regan pulled away.

"Uh-uh-uh, not yet," she said. My heart sank in frustration.

Regan slowly poured the remaining champagne over my pussy. I pulled against the restraints, digging my heels into the mattress and lifting my pelvis off the bed, trying to direct the stream of champagne onto my clit.

Regan let out a low moan. "Your pussy is so beautiful," she whispered as she bent down and licked the champagne from my thighs, working her way up. Her tongue outlined me, circling closer and closer, teasing my hard clit.

Excitement shot through my body as I felt the warm softness of her tongue finally caress my clit. She lapped and sucked hungrily at the champagne. Regan's soft full lips covered my pussy as her tongue stroked my throbbing clit, bringing me closer to orgasm. Suddenly, as if sensing I was on the brink, Regan shoved two fingers deep inside my pussy.

"Me or the bottle?"

"I love your fingers," I moaned. "Fuck me with your fingers."

After only a few long deep thrusts, my vagina quaked around her fingers and my orgasm surged through me.

Regan slid the bandanna off my eyes, reached up and unhitched the bungee cords. She rested her head on my chest, savoring the quiet after the storm. The room was dim and thick with the sweet smell of white roses and sex. Off in the distance, fireworks exploded.

I turned to Regan, gently kissed her soft, warm lips, and whispered, "Happy Fourth of July."